"I want to kiss you, Esmeralda."

Her arms were already circling around his neck. "If we're going to do this, just do it, Rodrigo."

He crushed his mouth on hers and the world fell away. It was like not a single day had passed since they'd last done this. She pressed herself to him as he peppered her neck with fluttering kisses. Somewhere in the back of her mind she knew this was the height of stupidity, that they were both being reckless. That if anyone found out about this, she would probably sink her chances to get approved by the board. But it was so hard to think when he was whispering intoxicatingly delicious things in Spanish. *Preciosa, amada...mia.*

It was foolish for him to call her his, and what was worse, she reveled in it.

"I can't get enough of you, Esmeralda. I never was able to."

* * *

One Week to Claim It All by Adriana Herrera is part of the Sambrano Studios series.

Dear Reader,

Growing up I could not get enough of romance novels and telenovelas. Sinking into one of those high-drama love stories could help me escape for a few hours into a world where people had thrilling and glamorous lives.

I imagined that those fabulous characters looked like me and could come from a Caribbean island just like I did. To be able to write Sambrano Studios, a series about a Dominican family at the helm of a television empire, has been an absolute delight—teenage me would be ecstatic!

The Sambranos are a family whose passions run high and their many secrets are deeply hidden. They're dreamers and strivers, and boy, do they love drama. Rodrigo and Esmeralda, the first couple in the series, have a *history*. Esmeralda is the illegitimate daughter of the patriarch of the Sambrano family, and Rodrigo is his protégé. They were in love once, but Rodrigo's put his ambitions before Esmeralda, and now she's the only thing standing in the way of him claiming his place as CEO of Sambrano Studios.

I hope you enjoy this first story in the Sambrano Studios series!

Happy reading!

Adriana

ADRIANA HERRERA

ONE WEEK TO CLAIM IT ALL

Recycling programs for this product may not exist in your area.

ISBN-13: 978-1-335-23295-3

One Week to Claim It All

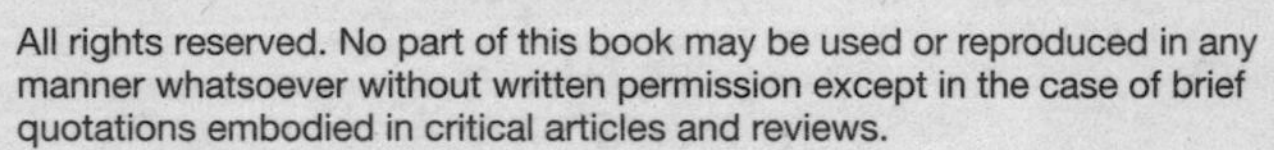

This edition published by arrangement with Harlequin Books S.A.

For questions and comments about the quality of this book, please contact us at CustomerService@Harlequin.com.

Harlequin Enterprises ULC
22 Adelaide St. West, 40th Floor
Toronto, Ontario M5H 4E3, Canada
www.Harlequin.com

Printed in U.S.A.

Adriana was born and raised in the Caribbean, but for the last fifteen years has let her job (and her spouse) take her all over the world. She loves writing stories about people who look and sound like her people, getting unapologetic happy endings. Her Dreamers series has received starred reviews from *Publishers Weekly* and *Booklist* and has been featured by the *Today* show on NBC, *Entertainment Weekly*, *O Magazine*, NPR, *Library Journal*, the *New York Times* and the *Washington Post*. She's a trauma therapist in New York City, working with survivors of domestic and sexual violence.

Books by Adriana Herrera

Harlequin Desire

Sambrano Studios

One Week to Claim It All

Carina Press

The Dreamers series

American Dreamer
American Fairytale
American Love Story
American Sweethearts
American Christmas

Dating in Dallas

Here to Stay

Visit her Author Profile page at Harlequin.com, or adrianaherreraromance.com, for more titles.

You can also find Adriana Herrera on Facebook, along with other Harlequin Desire authors, at Facebook.com/harlequindesireauthors.

To my mother and my tías: Miguelina,
Yudelka, Patria, Rebeca and Francis.
To me, you will always be the embodiment of
glamour, resilience and fierceness.

One

Esmeralda Sambrano-Peña leaned on the door to the small Washington Heights apartment she shared with her mother and took a moment to catch her breath. She could hear the excited chatter and laughter coming from inside, and the image of her mother and her three aunties holding their weekly get-together brought a tired smile to her face. Her tías and their penchant for neighborhood gossip and salacious jokes always managed to put her in a good mood. And after an extremely long and disappointing day it was comforting to hear familiar voices.

Her smile flagged when she realized she'd have to tell her mother, in front of her tías, that her project had been turned down. Again. Esmeralda sighed and tried to regroup with her body resting against the door. This rejection had hurt more than the others because she'd come so close. The TV series pilot she'd been trying to sell for almost two years had been inches away from actually getting produced. But at the last minute the producers had backed out, claiming the subject matter didn't have wide commercial appeal. Esme let out a frustrated huff as she put the key in the door and pushed it open.

"Hola, Mami!" she called tiredly from the narrow hallway leading to their small living room, while she took off her shoes and hung her jacket on the rack by the door. The apartment wasn't big, but it was enough space for them. Two bedrooms, with a living room and kitchen, on Riverside Drive was real estate gold in New York City. Esme flinched at the memory of how they'd ended up in the apartment she and her mother shared. Thinking about the reasons they'd been forced to move here in the first place still filled her with anger, even ten years later.

"Mija, the tías are here," her mother called loudly, as if Esme wasn't only a few feet away.

She shook her head, a smile tugging at her lips, as she stepped into the living room and found the four older women sprawled on the sectional couch, each with a glass of wine in hand. They were dressed to the nines, as always. To her mother and her aunts, leaving the house without a perfectly put together outfit and full makeup wasn't even an option.

"Ladies." She walked over and dutifully kissed

each one on the cheek. They were supposed to be discussing self-help books. But each week the affirmations and book talk lasted about thirty minutes, and the rest of the time was dedicated to downing chilled Moscato and gossiping about the latest news in the neighborhood or back home in the Dominican Republic.

"I see the book conversation is going well," she teased, taking a seat between her mother and her aunt Rebeca.

"What did they say?" Ivelisse asked, ignoring the comment about the neglected books on the coffee table. And of course the mere mention of her production meeting had the rest of the tías perking up. As soon as Esme sat down, she noticed that her mother looked a bit tense. Her usual cheerful expression was tentative, like she was anticipating trouble. She probably suspected Esme's meeting had been a bust.

Esme closed her eyes and shook her head, feeling defeated. "They passed on it." Words of encouragement quickly followed from all directions. Her mom threw an arm around her and her tías all shuffled around so they could pat her on the leg or the arm in an effort to reassure her.

"Their loss, mija. One day those dummies will wise up to your brilliance, and when they do, it'll be too late." Esme opened her eyes to find her tía Rebeca looking thunderous. She had always been Esme's number-one fan. Even back when Esme would make short films on her phone about events in the neighborhood, Rebeca would always sit down and watch, fully focused on her creations. She never hesitated to give her serious feedback.

"Thanks, Tía," Esme said wearily. She was grateful for their love and support. But she was too exhausted to go into the nonsense reasons the producers gave her for passing. "Enough about me. What else is going on—anything exciting happen today?"

To Esme's surprise they didn't push her to share more about her meeting. Instead every one of them shifted their expectant gazes to Esme's mom, who in turn got that look she only had when she was about to hit Esme with a strong dose of the Dominican guilt trip. She braced herself. "Qué pasó, Mami?"

Ivelisse didn't answer immediately, making a show of leaning over to get something that was sitting on the table. The energy in the room changed as soon as Ivelisse grabbed the white envelope. The tías all had their eyes on the piece of paper like it was a ticking bomb. For some reason Esme noticed that the vintage Tank Française watch Ivelisse never took off glinted in the light of the small lamp on the table. The gold Cartier watch had been a gift from Esme's father. And even after everything he'd done, Ivelisse cared for it as if it was a rare treasure. "This came for you today, mija," her mother said, bringing her out of her thoughts.

Esme narrowed her eyes at the name on the upper left corner of the envelope. She recognized it as the attorney who was handling her father's estate. She took it from her mother, noticing it had been slit open. "Mami," she chastised as she pulled the paper out. Ivelisse just lifted a shoulder, not even attempting contrition.

"It's happening tomorrow, Esmeralda."

Her mother didn't have to say what. Esmeralda already knew.

There in large black font at the very top of the expensive stationery were the words FINAL NOTICE. Eleven months and twenty-seven days had passed since her estranged father's death. Since she'd learned that, to the horror of his wife and his other children, he'd left a provision in his will to make Esmeralda the president and CEO of the television studio he'd turned into a billion-dollar empire. His last wish was to leave the daughter he'd barely acknowledged for most of her life at the helm of his company. Esme could still not quite believe it herself, and had done her best to ignore it whenever her mother had tried to show her the notices that had come every month since her father's death. But she hadn't turned it down, either, and now her time to decide was almost up.

Patricio Sambrano had started small in the '70s, producing some radio dramas and news shows in Spanish for the Latinx community in New York City. The shows became an instant sensation, and with the vision that would make him a legend in the entertainment industry, he soon realized what his people wanted was to see their stories on the small screen.

He hustled and harnessed old friendships on the island and across the US, and over the next fifteen years he brought Latinx life to American television. He'd been innovative, gutsy, political and unapologetic about showcasing the culture, and the end result had been Sambrano Studios, the first all-Spanish, all-color network in the United States.

Her father built something out of nothing with his ingenuity and raw talent. An Afro-Dominican man with barely a sixth-grade education had done all that. But as sharp as Patricio had been with his business, his personal life had been messy and undisciplined. Esmeralda herself was the result of one of the more chaotic times in Patricio's life. Only weeks after becoming engaged to the daughter of a Dominican financier, he married her—consolidating his ability to expand the studio's interests. It was a bold move that gave him the resources he needed to fully realize his dreams. It had been a surprise for everyone. Especially Esmeralda's mother, who had been in a relationship with Patricio for almost five years and only found out about the wedding when she heard about it on the Sambrano evening news. She'd been pregnant with Esmeralda when she realized that the man she loved had never intended to build a family with her.

When Ivelisse, devastated from his betrayal, finally told Patricio she was expecting, he told her he'd provide financially but he couldn't be a father to any child outside his marriage. And in that, at least, he'd been true to his word.

And then after twenty-nine years of treating her like she didn't exist, her father had overlooked his wife and his legitimate children to hand her the top position at Sambrano. Like that was supposed to make up for a lifetime of feeling like she didn't matter. To erase the humiliation she and her mother had suffered at his hands. The decades of being ignored or receiving messages from third parties because her father couldn't bother to pick up the phone when she called him.

Still, he *had* paid for the education that gave her the foundation to get a start in the industry and gain the experience she needed to run the studio. Because no matter how many times she'd told herself she didn't care what her father thought of her, when choosing a college she picked the University of Southern California because of their film and television program. When deciding on graduate school she went for an MBA with a focus in entertainment. Because she was a fool with daddy issues and despite being invisible to him most of her life, she still yearned for his approval.

But she'd never asked him for a job. And because she was also her mother's daughter, she'd wanted to show him that she didn't need him. She wanted to climb to the very top of his own industry without him. Not once did Esme give her father the satisfaction of hearing her ask for his help. She never thought he'd noticed and yet, his last wish was to entrust her with his legacy. She could do so much as president of Sambrano, but not at the price of selling herself out. Her pride had to be worth something.

And then again, maybe Patricio was just cashing in on the investment he'd made.

"Mi amor, where did you go?" Her mother's soft voice pierced through Esme's tumultuous thoughts. A pang of guilt and anticipation twisted in her gut as she looked at the paper again. It felt heavy in her hands: this could be the door to pursuing the vision she had for the future of Latinx television. But her father had never given her anything that didn't come at a cost, and the price had almost always been her pride. She'd learned long ago to always look for the strings whenever Patricio Sambrano was involved.

"Mami, this is a joke. Just another way for him to put me in my place. His kids and his wife won't stand for it."

Her mother and aunts responded to this with a choir of clucks and shaking heads. Her aunt Yocasta spoke before her mother could. "Mi niña, you know I've never had anything good to say about that cabrón." She didn't have to say who the cabrón was. Yocasta was never shy when it came to cursing Patricio Sambrano's name for the way he'd treated Esme and her mom. "But that baboso wouldn't risk his company to make a point. What he *would* do is go over the head of that bruja he married and put you in charge, if it's what he thought was best for the company."

Even her tía Zenaida, who usually let her three sisters opine while she silently observed, chimed in. "Patricio was always ruthless when it came to his business," she declared, while the others nodded. "If anything, I imagine he'd been keeping an eye on you and your hustle." She leaned over to tug one of Esme's curls, making her smile. "I hated that jackass, may he rest in peace." At that they all crossed themselves in unison, as if they had not all been cursing the man's name a second ago. Esme would've smiled at their ridiculousness, but she could barely move from the warring emotions coursing through her.

"For better or worse he always put that studio first," Zenaida said, which prompted a flurry of nods from the older women. "If he picked you to be the president and CEO it's because he thought you were right for the job."

"His wife is going to make my life a living hell," Esme said, unable to hide the real wariness in her voice. Carmelina Sambrano was not above humiliating her. But that got Ivelisse's back up.

"She can try, but you can stand up to her," her mother said with a confidence Esmeralda wished she felt. "And besides, you'll be in charge."

"I don't know, Mami." She hated that even thinking of being rejected by her father's wife and children made her feel small.

Ivelisse made another clucking noise and pulled

Esme closer. "Screw them. Go in there tomorrow and claim your place. Use them and this opportunity to do all the things you've been wanting to do but haven't gotten the chance to."

Esme's chest fluttered with an ember of hope and longing at her mother's words. Ivelisse was right, she'd been killing herself for the past five years—trying and failing to get her projects off the ground, but she could not get a break. Because her ideas weren't "commercial" enough, or relatable to the "mainstream" audience. She was tired of getting doors shut in her face because she refused to compromise. As head of Sambrano Studios she could make her dream come to life. Put shows out there that reflected all the faces of Latinx culture.

If she wasn't pushed out by Carmelina first.

"Mami, that woman is never going to let me stay. And I don't want to sink to her level." Ivelisse had been a wonderful mother, gentle and kind, but she was a fighter when it counted, and the mention of her old foe lit a fire behind her eyes.

"Carmelina won't know how to fight you, baby. That woman has never done a day of work in her life. When you go in there—smart, competent, full of fresh ideas—that board won't know what hit them." That ember was now a tiny flame fueled by the faith Esme's mother had in her. Still, she'd learned the hard way not to trust anything that came from her father.

"But won't the board have someone picked out

already? Someone that doesn't come with the drama that I will certainly cause?"

Her mother averted her eyes at her question and *that* gave Esme pause. "Mami?" she asked wearily as she scanned the paper in her hands again, looking for whatever her mother wasn't saying. And when she got to the very last paragraph she understood. Her body flashed hot and cold, just from reading that name. There in black and white was the last push she needed to jump right into an ocean of bad decisions.

"Him?" she asked tersely, and from the corner of her eye she saw her mother flinch.

Rodrigo Almanzar, her father's protégé and the person who for years had been the only tie she had to Patricio. The man she'd given her heart and her body to only to have him betray her when she needed him most. The man whose very name could still make her ache with longing and tremble with fury. How could it still hurt so much after all this time?

She felt tired. Tired of this damn thing hanging over her head. Tired of all the complicated feelings she had about everything having to do with Sambrano Studios. Especially when it came to the tall, brawny, arrogant bastard who was probably hoping she'd do the very thing she'd been considering. Let her pride and her baggage make her decision for her.

And she might have, if *he* wasn't the one who'd end up as president and CEO. She wouldn't do it out of greed, or even to appease her mother, but she would do it out of spite. Rodrigo had betrayed her just so he could continue as her father's lapdog. Now she'd take the thing he'd sold his soul for…just when he thought he finally had it.

"Actually," she said, standing up, already feeling the fire in her gut that usually preceded her doing ill-advised things. "You're right." The four women in her living room were all looking at her with varying degrees of anticipation. "I've been saying for years that if given the chance to shoot my shot I wouldn't hesitate to take it. This isn't exactly how I'd hoped to get it, but now that I do, I'm not wasting it. Tomorrow, Sambrano will get its new president and CEO."

Her mother eyed Esme with suspicion, probably guessing what had been the deciding factor for her change of heart, while her aunt Yocasta crowed with delight, "Ay, Ivelisse, what I wouldn't give to see the look on Carmelina's face when Esme walks into that boardroom tomorrow."

Esme smiled wryly at her aunt, but her mind was already racing toward the other shocked face she was looking forward to seeing.

Two

This is bittersweet, Rodrigo Almanzar thought as he smoothed a hand over his Hermès tie and the jacket of the slate Brioni suit he'd ordered special for this day. Finally taking the helm of the company he'd been working for since he was sixteen years old warranted splurging fifty grand. Even if this wasn't how he'd envisioned things happening.

He wished him taking the job at the head of Sambrano Studios didn't come as a result of losing Patricio. A flash of grief, and the usual tangle of emotions that his old mentor evoked in him, dulled the electric anticipation he'd been feeling all week. Patricio had been more than his mentor; he'd been his dad's best friend and his family's savior once upon a time.

The man had taught Rodrigo everything he knew about the business he loved. Patricio had many shortcomings, and over the years the things Rodrigo had seen him do bordered on outright cruelty. But even when Patricio seemed to be hell-bent on alienating everyone in his life, his bond with Rodrigo had remained strong.

Well, there had been that one night. The moment when Rodrigo had bartered with everything he had, and he'd gotten what he wanted. Then lost everything anyways.

Yeah, no matter what the gossips liked to say about Rodrigo's "special treatment" from Patricio, the man had never pulled his punches. When he was in one of his moods, anyone could get the brunt of it. But Rodrigo had learned how to maneuver the older man, and even when he knew he should've quit, his loyalty had kept him working for Sambrano. Even after it had cost Rodrigo the woman he loved. *Loyal to a fault*, his mother had always said, and maybe when it came to Patricio it was true.

One night in those last days, when the once tall and powerful man had been emaciated by illness, he'd confessed that Rodrigo reminded him of himself. That he'd turned into the kind of man he'd wished he could've been. Rodrigo shook his head, dismissing that, but Patricio's eyes had been full of affection and pride. The same affection and pride that had kept Rodrigo tethered to his desk even when he'd hated the things Patricio had done. When staying in this company really felt like it had cost Rodrigo his soul.

And that line of thinking brought him right to the one person he'd been avoiding thinking about for days. For weeks, really. Since the estate executor had made the last attempt to contact Esmeralda Sambrano-Peña to ask if she would be honoring her father's last wishes and taking over Sambrano Studios. Rodrigo didn't believe in skirting the rules, even when there was good reason. But after twelve months of having the executor's calls ignored he figured that was answer enough. No matter how much he wanted to officially be named president and CEO, he'd done his due diligence. And today no one could say he had manipulated the circumstances. Hell, he'd gone out of his way to make sure Esmeralda got the chance to claim the position.

After wrangling with the likes of Carmelina Sambrano for the past year Rodrigo was more certain than ever that he needed to be in charge. Esmeralda didn't have the temperament to deal with that viper and her pack of cronies. Patricio's widow would be waiting in the wings for her to fail so she could take her late husband's life's work and sell it for pieces to the highest bidder. No, sweet and soft-spoken Esmeralda would not be up for the dogfight this was going to be.

He cleared his throat as he looked around the room. Sambrano's headquarters in Midtown Manhattan were housed in an Art Deco building from the 1920s. Patricio had all the original moldings and wood painstakingly restored, but this boardroom was the crown jewel of the executive floor. A massive space overlooking Central Park. The walls were all done in wood paneling that gave the room a warm feel, even if the meetings as of late had been anything but. The showpiece in the room was the table, a hundred-year-old behemoth that sat twenty-four people. It was a perfect solid oak oval, with an Italian rose marble top. Patricio had acquired it at an estate sale in the '70s on a whim and kept it in storage until he grew his business enough to display it. It was ostentatious now, but when Patricio had purchased it, the studio only getting off the ground, it must have seemed recklessly arrogant. But his mentor had made good on the promise of that table. He'd built an empire befitting its grandeur, and Rodrigo would be damned if he let it all be laid to waste by his family's greed.

The sumptuous burgundy leather chairs were occupied by all ten members of the Sambrano Studios executive board, in addition to Carmelina and her two children, Perla and Onyx. As vicious as Carmelina was when it came to her husband's money, her children didn't seem to care in the slightest what happened to their family legacy. Perla seemed perennially preoccupied with her travel plans and not much else and as for Onyx…he only remembered the studio existed when he needed it to get invitations to celebrity parties.

Useless. All of them.

But that was just fine. Rodrigo would be in charge, and he knew what he needed to do, had been meticulously planning it for years—with Esmeralda as a no-show it seemed the one snag had been smoothed out. He got to his feet, suddenly feeling the urgency of getting the meeting going. In theory Patricio's heiress had another hour to claim her place, but by the time they got to that part of the agenda they would be well past the window.

"Ladies and gentlemen." He made sure to project his voice and it resounded across the room. Soon even Perla and Onyx were peeling their eyes off their phones and turning their attention to Rodrigo. "Thank you for coming today. I can't say that this isn't bittersweet."

Rodrigo stopped to take a breath, surprised by the wave of emotion tightening his chest. "Patricio was like a father to me…" He ignored what sounded like a scoff coming from the direction where Carmelina was sitting and focused on the people in the room that, like him, were concerned with not seeing a lifetime of work be flushed down the drain. "And he has left enormous shoes to fill. I couldn't be prouder to officially take the helm of Sambrano and hope that together we can create a future for the studio that he would be proud of."

His pulse quickened as the words he'd just uttered sank in. This was really happening. Sixteen years of working tirelessly, of sacrificing his personal life for this company, was paying off with what had always been his goal: being president and CEO of Sambrano Studios. He might not have the last name, but he'd given everything to this company, and now he would be the one to take it into the future.

Some of the people in this room—hell, people all over the industry—loved to whisper about "the forbidding" next-in-line at Sambrano. Joked that Patricio had Rodrigo's emotions surgically removed before giving him the chief content officer position. But Rodrigo let that slide right off his Brioni-clad shoulders. They talked because he'd persevered, had triumphed when so many others failed. He'd been the youngest CCO in the industry eight years ago when he got the position, and when he took over as interim CEO—after Patricio's illness had forced him to step down a year ago—he'd become one of the highest-paid Latinos in all of entertainment. He was a millionaire dozens of times over in his own right, and now was head of a billion-dollar company.

They hated him because they wanted to be where he was. And he would not apologize for how he'd gotten here.

"Sambrano has always been unique in the business and my plan is to continue that tradition," he continued, and was pleased to hear sounds of approval from some in the room. Others remained silent. Then again this was a contentious line of conversation. The topic of what direction Sambrano would take in the next decade had been hotly contested. Some wanted to keep things as they were and others wanted to think more innovatively, to be more competitive in this new era of streaming and global programming. One more challenge he'd had to tackle immediately.

The voices around the room were interrupted when the door to the boardroom suddenly burst open. The entrance was off to the right, beyond Rodrigo's range of vision, but the varying looks of shock from those facing the door gave him an inkling of who it was before he turned around.

"Sorry I'm late. The trains uptown were a mess today." The various surprised gasps, and in Carmelina's case, something very close to a roar, went a long way to confirm the newcomer's identity. Ten years was not such a long time that he wouldn't remember the voice of the person who had meant the most to him at one time in his life. The only person that elicited regret in him. The self-confidence was new, but he'd recognize Esmeralda's raspy tone anywhere. He'd always thought she sounded like she was hoarse from laughing too hard or singing too loud. She didn't sound like she was laughing now.

By the time he turned, she was already in front of him. This was not the twenty-one-year-old girl he'd last seen the summer Patricio broke his daughter's heart—and him, too; Rodrigo had broken her heart, too. She'd been beautiful back then. Always too beautiful for him to resist. With her lavish curls that fell around her shoulders in a palette of brown and gold, and that flawless skin, like Dominican mahogany. But her eyes had always been his perdition, those big hazel orbs that always saw a little too much. He'd made mistakes with this woman that would haunt him for the rest of his life. Too many to rehash right now, especially when her arrival was about to wreak havoc on his carefully laid plans.

This was not the unsure, sensitive girl he fell for all those years ago. The one who had looked at him like he was the man of her dreams. The one whose soft body he'd lost himself in again and again. The woman standing here exuded confidence and at the moment was staring at him with open hostility. This Esmeralda was self-possessed, and she knew exactly the effect she was having on him.

"Rodrigo."

He'd never known one word could carry with it so much disdain, and that was a good reminder he had to snap out of it and get his head in the game. He had a history with Esmeralda Sambrano-Peña, but he could not let that cloud his judgment. He'd once let his feelings for her almost ruin his career, and he would not make the same mistake again. No matter how much her presence rattled him. He should have expected this. Seeing her had been a possibility hanging over his head since nearly a year ago, when the executor of Patricio's will gathered them all in this same room and dropped the bomb of the century on them.

And yet, his reaction to her still caught him by

surprise. Every instinct he had incited him to get closer. But as he took her in, the defiant eyes, the determined set of her mouth, he at least saw things clearly. He could not underestimate this woman, not if he wanted to keep those three letters attached to his name.

"Started without me, I see," she said, trying to provoke him. Sarcasm dripped from her every word. Her full mouth set in a hard line. Her eyes, which in the past had looked at him with such adoration, now cool and distant. As if she could see right through him. She'd come dressed to kill today. Her black suit fit her like a glove, and even now, when he suspected her arrival was about to upend everything, he could not help but notice the luscious curves of her body.

In the past ten years Rodrigo had told himself a million times he could handle her disdain. That he'd made the right decision in letting her go. That if she hated him for it, it had been worth it, for both their sakes. But now, after just a mere moment of having her back in his space, he knew he'd been lying to himself all along. The truth was that he had a weakness for Esmeralda. And men like him could not afford to be ruled by their vulnerabilities. His father had been like that, unable to keep himself in check, undisciplined, and it had cost their family everything. Rodrigo had promised himself years ago he would never follow in those footsteps. Rodrigo did not allow his passions to rule his head, even if it meant appearing ruthless to the one person in the world he never wanted to hurt. He'd done it once before. It had almost killed him, but he'd survived, and now he'd do it again if that was what it took.

"I never took you for one for theatrics, Esmeralda." He sounded like an absolute bastard, but it had to be done. This was not a game, and if Esme wanted this position, he would treat her like he would any competitor.

Her head snapped in his direction at the sound of his voice, and when her gaze landed on him again her expression went from cold to mutinous. Esmeralda had not let bygones be bygones, it seemed. All the better to keep himself in check. And if his stomach lurched and his blood rushed between his temples with a roar, well, that was just frustration at having his plans disrupted. Nothing more.

Rodrigo had learned the hard way not to let emotions creep into his professional life. And that was what this was for him, his job, not some family drama. Carmelina and her children, even Esmeralda, could throw tantrums now, but Rodrigo could not afford outbursts. And he certainly could not spend another second fixating on Esmeralda's mobile, generous mouth and all the ways he knew she could use it to undo him.

She waved a hand at him and turned to the seat he'd just emptied. "So testy, Rodrigo." She clicked her tongue, as derision dripped from every word out of her mouth. "You're all in your feelings because I came to ruin your coronation? I guess it didn't occur to anyone that I might actually be up for taking this job." Her tone could melt the paint off the walls, but he would not take that bait.

"That's okay," she goaded, turning to Carmelina Sambrano, who was practically vibrating in her seat at the far end of the table. "I'm happy to fill everyone in, as soon as I officially assume my position as president and CEO." With that she went to the head of the table, the very seat Rodrigo had been about to occupy, and sat down.

"Are you people going to let this travesty happen?" The widow's cry of unbridled outrage reminded Rodrigo there were other people in the room. And he'd had just about enough of the Sambranos and their need to turn *everything* into a telenovela. He stepped up to Esme, determined to get this farce under control. He'd had to put up with this for sixteen years. The Sambranos and their chaos. Their backbiting and their drama. As if this was all about them, like there weren't thousands of workers depending on the people in this room for their livelihoods. He had no idea what game Esmeralda was playing at, but he was not putting up with any of this.

"Esmeralda, what the hell do you think you're doing?"

For a second her mask slipped. For a moment shorter than the blink of an eye he saw that the way he spoke to her surprised her. And he almost hesitated, ensnared by the urge to soothe her. To fix this for Esmeralda. But he reminded himself that was not his job. "You have to know this isn't appropriate," he ground out, forcing himself to keep an even tone. "That there are timelines. There are *procedures*. You don't understand—"

"No," she said, curtly lifting herself from the seat she'd just commandeered. "*You* don't understand." She was standing so close he could see a tiny bead of perspiration gather between her breasts, and he hated himself for the throb of lust that coursed through him. "I'm taking my position as president and CEO of Sambrano and if that affects your or anyone else's plans…" That she directed at her half-siblings, who were still sitting, mouths gaping. "That's your problem, *not mine*. Now, where in the agenda were we?" With that she placidly sat down, leaving him there like a six-foot-two-inch-tall office ornament.

That arrogance, it should've incensed him. But, dammit, instead a wave of raw need almost made him stumble. His hands itched to touch her, to take that mouth and find out if it still tasted as sweet as he remembered. But he smothered that urge down to ashes. This was what he excelled at, after all. Locking down and repressing every emotion. In the last days of her illness, his mother told him he'd lost himself to this job, that she didn't recognize the man he'd become. And it would've hurt if it wasn't the truth, but Rodrigo long ago had understood that denying reality was harder work than just learning to live with it.

"I don't plan to lose this game, Esmeralda. I'm

sure you've learned a lot about the industry scouting film locations." The loathing in her eyes would have made a lesser man cower, but Rodrigo thrived in moments like this. "There's a very long distance between thinking you know how to do something and actually doing it, and *I* know *everything* about this company."

He saw the moment that self-doubt crept in, when his words started edging out the confidence she'd walked in with. But like he'd told himself over and over again, that was not his problem. He'd been preparing for this moment his whole professional life and he would be damned if he let it slip away now. No matter how much Esmeralda Sambrano-Peña got under his skin.

Three

Keep it together, Esmeralda. You can handle this.

That was the mantra that had been going through her head since the moment she stepped through Sambrano Studios' front doors. She'd known what would happen in the boardroom would be intimidating. She'd even expected it to be outright confrontational. But what she hadn't expected was how unsettling it would be to be in this building and not have Rodrigo on her side. In the rare occasions over the years when Esme had been forced to come see her father, Rodrigo had always made a point of being there for her.

Arturo, Rodrigo's father, had been a good friend of Esme's mother. No, Arturo had been more than a friend—he'd stood up for Ivelisse when Carmelina made up lies about her. When Carmelina tried to push Esme out of the picture, Arturo had been her champion. And when Arturo was gone, Rodrigo took on that role. For years he was her only channel of communication to Patricio Sambrano. He'd been her rock for a long time, and then he'd been her lover. Her first everything, and he'd thrown it all away, out of his misguided loyalty to her father.

She breathed through pain that cut off the air in her lungs as she considered him. She hated that his betrayal still hurt her. And she despised that even after everything that happened between them she still wanted him. She didn't attempt to hide that she was looking at him. More than looking, she was inspecting him from head to toe. He was still heart-stoppingly handsome with that bronzed skin that seemed almost lit from within. The rough, coarse curls that he kept austerely short, and placated with exacting care. His full, generous lips were in a terse, unhappy line, and she wanted more than anything to press her mouth to them. Dark eyes to match his mood, and still she could see there was more than anger in those chocolate-brown depths, glints of desire that he couldn't hide from her. But she tamped that thought down mercilessly and focused on Rodrigo's not-so-charming attributes. Like his fastidiousness about his appearance. She could almost bet the suit he was wearing had been reserved for this day months in advance.

To all the world Rodrigo Almanzar was the unfeeling, ambitious television wunderkind. But she knew that behind all that stoic demeanor the man she'd loved was a little vain about that tall, imposing body. And she couldn't deny that he'd worked very hard for it. He'd been a point guard in high school and college. Esmeralda had gone to see him play with her mother, who had been his mom's best friend. She'd loved him then, too, but it was a different kind of love. She'd looked up to him, admired how he'd been able to balance working and going to school. That he supported his mother when Arturo gambled away everything they had. And after, when she was in college and he was fresh out of grad school and working full-time for her dad, it had turned into something different. But that happiness had been fleeting and in the end he'd broken her heart.

And that was the one thing she could not forget today—how ruthless Rodrigo could be. How on the day she'd learned her father had evicted her mother from the apartment Esme had lived in all her life, instead of helping, Rodrigo told her he could not afford distractions, and she—their relationship—was a distraction. And that was why she would never forgive him.

She opened her mouth to let him know in no uncertain terms she would not falter in taking this job from him—that she'd also learned to be merciless—when someone called her name from the other side of the room.

“Esmeralda. Turn around and look at me.” She hadn’t seen or heard from Carmelina Sambrano in a very long time, but the woman’s voice was not one she’d ever forget. Esmeralda took a moment as she fought to keep the mask of impassive disdain she’d been wearing from slipping off. To keep from letting Carmelina’s words get to her. She knew the woman was vicious and would not hesitate to humiliate her. The bastard child Carmelina had tried to erase from Patricio’s life for almost thirty years was now here threatening everything she held dear. But Carmelina could rage at her, call her names and make a scene. It would not change the contents of Patricio’s will.

“I’m happy to turn around,” Esmeralda drawled as she moved to face her father’s widow. “I want you to take a good look at me, Carmelina. You’ve worked so hard at pretending I don’t exist, you may have started believing it. But it’s going to be a little hard to ignore me now, isn’t it?”

Her father’s widow inhaled sharply, her platinum updo bobbing as the woman clearly scrambled for control. “You will not get away with this,” Carmelina hissed through clenched teeth.

“We’ll just have to see, won’t we?” She knew she was pushing the older woman, could see in her eyes she was on the verge of exploding, but Esmeralda had put up with too much over the years to back down. “Things are going to be a little different from now on.”

For an instant she thought she saw a glimmer of

something like pride in Rodrigo's eyes. Bolstered by the knowledge that Carmelina had no power over her, Esme ran a hand over the black tailored pantsuit she'd worn. She looked down at the Gucci stilettos on her feet, from the outlet in Peekskill, but, hey, they still made her look like a million bucks. She might have never been in the bosom of the Sambrano family, but she could play the part if she had to. Her mother had made sure of that.

She felt the weight of every eye in the room trained in her direction. "So," she said to no one in particular. "How are we going to do this?"

Despite having never been inside this boardroom before, she knew every person around the table. Not just because it was her father's company, but because Sambrano's board was made up of a who's who of the biggest Latinx names in the business. And then there were the ones sitting here because of their *last name*. Perla and Onyx Sambrano. She hadn't seen them in person since they were kids, and yet from the first glance she could see so much of herself in their faces. The same nose and thick eyebrows. Perla even had the smatter of freckles on the apple of her cheeks Esme had.

"Miss Sambrano."

Esmeralda's gaze shifted to the source of a new person trying to catch her attention. She recognized Octavio Nuñez the moment she laid eyes on him. The man had been an institution in Spanish television for decades. He'd started at the studio not long after the network began broadcasting nationally. He'd been the first Spanish-speaking evening news anchor in American television history. And now he was on the board of Sambrano—the chair of the board to be exact. He was also Carmelina's cousin and Esme had no idea what to expect from him.

"Sambrano-Peña" she clarified as she held her head up, eyes focused on the man who had stood up to address her. His expression was guarded—not friendly, but not contentious, either. She wanted to shift her gaze to Carmelina and see how *she* was looking at her cousin. Esmeralda shifted uncomfortably as the man studied her, unsure what to expect, when she heard a whisper from behind her.

"They hate each other. Octavio's on whatever side Carmelina isn't."

Rodrigo.

Esmeralda dipped her head, acknowledging what he'd said, but didn't respond. Octavio was speaking again. "Welcome. This is a surprise. After all our attempts to contact you went unanswered the board assumed you weren't interested."

Carmelina made an attempt to get up, but something held her back. And then Esme noticed Perla's hand on her mother's arm. Octavio did not spare his cousin a glance, his attention on Esmeralda. He pointed at the chair that she'd gotten up from in a gesture that she sit down.

"Your father's wish to have you assume the role of president and CEO of the studio was a surprise to all of us." There were some sounds of agreement around the table. Some of them even sounded like encouraging ones. "You *are* young," he said, but his expression was not unkind. "However, your experience in television and film is impressive." This time Octavio did send a look toward Carmelina. A withering one. "It's hardly a secret that in the last few years Patricio didn't see eye to eye with the board on a few things, but for the most part we're all invested in doing what's best for Sambrano." Rodrigo had been right—there was no love lost between those two, not if the vicious glares they directed at each other were any indication.

"That being said..." The throat clearing from most of the people around the table told her the other shoe was about to drop. "Your father gave the board the liberty to make some stipulations around how to assess if you are the right person for the job." Esmeralda could hear the hesitation in Octavio's voice and dread sank through her like a ball of lead. Whatever those "stipulations" were, she would not enjoy them. "And there's something else. Patricio asked that his personal stake in Sambrano Studios—twenty-five percent of the total shares to be exact—be held in a trust until you decided to comply with his wishes."

"What does that mean?" she asked in confusion, no longer caring about how she sounded or looked. She was out of her depth, and everyone in this room probably realized it.

Octavio gave her a reassuring smile and picked

up a folder, which he slid toward her. "That means that you are now the owner of twenty-five percent of Sambrano Studios. Fifty percent is held by your siblings and Mrs. Sambrano holds the remaining shares." Esmeralda was glad she was already sitting down because if she weren't she would've probably been knocked on her ass. This was a billion-dollar company; those shares had to be worth hundreds of millions. And right after that thought, it dawned on her that of course her father would only give those shares to her if she complied with what he wanted. Because nothing was ever free with Patricio.

Awful as that was, the shares still gave her some leverage, and she'd take it. Another round of throat clearing erupted and Esme noticed that by now, Perla was almost forcibly keeping her mother in her seat. But Carmelina's mouth was working fine.

"This is outrageous. Someone must have influenced Patricio. He was not in his right mind at the end. This is the only explanation!" she yelled, pounding her small fist on the table. "She has nothing to do with Sambrano! You can't do this. I'm trying to protect my children's rightful legacy! I will not allow this imposter to be the face of my husband's company." Carmelina's mouth was twisted into an ugly sneer as she yelled. "I'd rather see it burn to the ground than let you sit in that office."

Esme's heart hammered in her chest and her stomach churned at the loathing dripping from every word Carmelina uttered. The woman had always despised her. Even when Esmeralda was only a child she'd gone out of her way to be cruel. On the few occasions she'd been invited to her father's house, Carmelina had made her life miserable until her mother had stopped sending her altogether. But Esme was not that little girl anymore, and she was not letting her father's widow take one more thing from her. So she leaned in, both hands on the table, and spoke directly to the woman who had caused her and her mother so much pain.

"It's not up to you. They're *my* father's wishes." Carmelina twisted her mouth at the mention of Esme's parentage. "I didn't ask to be his child any more than your children did, and yet here I am. So, we're just all going to learn to live with the fact that I'm now part of Sambrano Studios. Whether you like it or not, this is *my* legacy, too." Esme didn't miss the looks of approval she saw on some of the faces in the room as she leaned back. "Mr. Nuñez, you were saying?" She made sure she sounded placid and unbothered.

Octavio seemed to appreciate her approach. "Like I was saying, we're happy to see you appointed as president and CEO if we determine you are the best person for the job." He looked to Rodrigo, who Esme noticed sat up for whatever was coming next. "Here is how it's going to go. You have one week to present a five-year strategic plan for the studio. A week from today, we will meet here again."

Esme's skin prickled with excitement even as she

wondered how she'd be able to pull that off in one week. It took her months to prepare her pitch for her pilot and now she would have to deliver a strategic plan for an entire network that had dozens of programming tracks in just seven days?

She squared her shoulders at the challenge, her head high, knowing this was part of the test. If she complained, if she asked the board for more time, it would count against her. And now she had something to prove.

"I can do that," she assured the man.

"Excellent." Octavio certainly did not seem like a foe now, and she could use a friend or two in her corner.

"I'll need a space to work and access to the archives and programming schedule. I'll also need to receive briefings from each production studio." Blood rushed to her ears as her mind raced with all the things she needed to prepare. "Including film. I know they're on the West Coast, but we'll need to set up a conference call with the different heads of departments." She pulled out her phone to make some notes and stood up, ready to get started.

"Esmeralda." Her head snapped up at the tone in Octavio's voice; something about the way he called her name made the hairs on the back of her neck stand up. "Rodrigo Almanzar, who has served as interim CEO for the past year and was our CCO for almost eight years prior to that, will be your go-to person as you prepare. He will also be consulting with you on the content we'd like to see."

No. No. *No.*

Her body ran hot and cold at that piece of news. This was it. The reason why Octavio had been all pleasant and calm about all this. They never intended her to take the position. This was all theatrics. They'd pretend they were giving her a chance while Rodrigo tripped her up every step of the way. This was the board covering their asses before they shut her out. *Of course* Rodrigo would help them do this to her; the board probably hatched this plan the moment they learned about Patricio's will. She fisted her hands, struggling to suffuse the hurt and anger boiling within her.

This was how it was in the boardroom. Low down dirty tricks and backstabbing. They expected her to tuck her tail between their legs and thank them for setting her up to fail. Well, she would show them. "If that's what the board wishes." Her voice was as cold as she could make it, and when she turned to Rodrigo she could hardly see him through her narrowed eyes. "I'm sure Mr. Almanzar will do his duty. He always does. No matter the consequences." She infused that with as much venom as she could, but it seemed he was not taking the bait.

"You can call me Rodrigo, Esmeralda." He was next to her, so close that she could swear she felt the heat radiating from him body.

"Only my friends call me Esmeralda, and you're not my friend," she said, before turning away.

Octavio cleared his throat, looking uncomfortable. "We trust that Rodrigo will do what is best for the studio." The finality in the man's voice told her there was no point in arguing. This was what she had to work with.

She turned her gaze to her former lover. His mouth was in that mutinous line again but she could see the hurt in his eyes. Her words had put it there. She dearly wished she didn't react to that knowledge. But more than anything, she wished that Rodrigo Almanzar was not who she would need to work with on this. Because beyond anything he was planning to do, her own feelings for him were her biggest liability.

She willed herself to feel nothing as she looked around the boardroom again, her eyes never stopping, not even on Carmelina's smug face. "I'll get to work then. I will see you all here in a week."

With that she strode out of the boardroom, Rodrigo hot on her heels. But if Esmeralda had learned one lesson from her mother it was that when life gave you lemons you made lemonade. She vowed to herself the next time she walked out of this room, she would be the new president and CEO of Sambrano Studios.

Four

Rodrigo followed Esmeralda out of the boardroom, his mind reeling from what had gone down in there. He'd had no idea this was the board's plan. Octavio had not been dead set against Patricio's request, but some in the board were furious about it. They'd told him they were going to activate a contingency plan in the event she actually showed up. This was the brilliant idea they'd come up with? Forcing him to be the one to walk her through this fiasco and take the brunt of her anger when things went sideways? Because she would mostly likely fail. Having industry experience did not translate to having the know-how to manage a billion-dollar studio.

And he would not pull punches when it came down to it.

And where the hell was she going?

"Esmeralda, wait," he called as she made a beeline away from the boardroom. "We need to talk."

"I need a minute, Rodrigo." She still wasn't facing him, but he could hear the tension in her shaky voice. His protective instincts immediately kicked in, urging him to reach for her. He'd always had a hard time keeping his head in the game when it came to this woman. Which was why over the next week he'd have to remind himself as much as necessary that Esmeralda was his competition. Just from those few minutes in the boardroom he knew it would be a grave mistake to not take her seriously.

Not that he had ever thought Esmeralda was anything but brilliant. But what she'd done today, that took guts. To walk into that boardroom and claim her place had to have been terrifying, but she'd done it and held her own. He respected that. And even now, when it felt like the stress of it all was enough to make him snap in two, it was hard to ignore the pulse of desire. And this was absolutely not the moment for any of that.

"Joya, espera." As he expected, that stopped her in her tracks. She turned on him, those leonine eyes flashing with fury.

"You don't get to call me that anymore, Rodrigo Almanzar." Her mouth was pursed, nostrils flaring as she glared at him.

It had been a low blow, he knew that, to use the nickname he used to call her all those years ago, when against his better judgment he'd gotten involved with Esmeralda. No, *involved* made it seem like it had been a fling, something that had run its course after a time. When in fact it had been earth-shattering, all-consuming, the thing that brought him almost to the brink of losing everything. But that was what she'd been: his jewel.

Patricio Sambrano had named his children after precious stones. Esmeralda, Onyx, Perla. And Esme *was* the first jewel in her father's life. But Patricio never knew how to care for her the way she deserved. He'd never been able to appreciate the gem he'd been given. But Rodrigo had. He'd loved her as a kid, been protective of her. Of the child who lived in the shadows of her father's life. And then he'd loved her as a woman, who even at twenty had had a clear sense of who she was. Ten years of hustling for a dream that seemed to stay constantly out of her reach had not dimmed her light. If anything, at thirty she shone even brighter.

At the moment the light in Esme's eyes was not warm, it was mutinous. He gestured to one of the small workrooms that were scattered around the studio. Private offices where the staff who worked in cubes could have a conference call or work on more sensitive material without disrupting others. "Let's talk in here." He would've taken her to his office, but since that was the office she was here gunning for, he figured they'd stay in neutral territory.

She wasn't moving, her feet firmly planted on the ground. "I'm not going anywhere with you." She pointed in the direction they'd both come from, her face pinched with fury. "You set all that up."

He considered her for a moment. The stubborn set of her shoulders, the defiant look in her eyes. Just beyond that there was a small quiver of lips, and a brittleness to her demeanor that told him this was getting to her. And if she was anyone else, he'd go in for the kill. He'd begin listing every reason why she would fail. How unprepared she was. But this *was* Esmeralda.

"I had no idea this was what they were planning." From her expression it was clear she didn't believe him, and he wished that didn't sting as much as it did. "Despite how you or the rest of the world may feel about me, I don't actually spend my day scheming about how to steal this company."

"You have no idea how I feel about anything," she said coldly, before turning on her heel and heading into one of the offices. His eyes instantly drifted to the curve of her waist and the swell of her backside as he walked in after her and closed the door.

Her smell filled the space. The same spicy fragrance of lemongrass and ginger that she'd been using for years. This was going to be an absolute fiasco, but not in the way Esmeralda thought. He was the problem, *his reaction to her* was the issue.

"I know you're angry, but you won't win by letting your emotions get to you."

She scoffed at that, but he ignored it. "And I resent the implication that I would play dirty. I would never stab you in the back like that, Esmeralda. You know—"

"What do I know?" she demanded, her expression thunderous. "That after you promised me a thousand times that you had my back, you cut me loose in a second? That in the end you chose him?" Her voice broke just the smallest bit on the last word—*him.*

He knew this was coming, but it still felt like a blow to his solar plexus, every ounce of oxygen escaping his lungs at once. He wanted to tell her the truth, explain how things had gone so terribly wrong that weekend so long ago. How Patricio had fallen for Carmelina's lies and scheming.

"I never—"

The anger and frustration coursing through him felt like molten lava in his veins, the need to tell her the truth almost shattering his self-control. But he couldn't. He swore he would never speak of how things went down, not even to defend himself from Esmeralda's loathing. What was the use? After all these years finally telling Esmeralda what really happened would only make things worse. Minutes, merely minutes of having her back in his life and the cold and controlled demeanor he was known for was tearing at his seams.

And yet, instead of leaving this room, going

somewhere he could get himself together, he moved toward her.

His nostrils flared, body tight with the need to touch her. To see if his caress still affected her like it used to. If his hands on her hair, his mouth on hers still made her melt. But that was not what they were to each other anymore. That part of them had been irrevocably broken. He'd thrown away his chance to have her like that.

"We can keep this professional. I want to be CEO of Sambrano Studios. I've worked for it. I even think I deserve it."

She opened her mouth to speak, but whatever she saw on his face made her pause. "But despite his faults, I respected your father and I would never interfere with his wishes. If you're the best person for the job, I won't stand in your way, but I won't give it to you, either." His back molars clenched, from the need to soothe the hurt he saw in her eyes from his words. "As a matter of fact, be prepared to fight like hell, because that's what I plan to do." No matter how much Esmeralda got to him, and she clearly could still undo him, he would not back down from this.

"I don't need you to give me anything." She practically spat out the words. "And I plan to fight for this, too."

She'd come closer with every word, and now they were only inches apart. He still towered over her. She was only a few inches above five feet, but what she lacked in stature she'd always more than made up for in personality.

"Oh, that I'm very clear on," he said bitterly. She'd turned down every attempt he'd made to reach out to her over the years. Rejected every effort from her father or him to help her get ahead in the industry. She was determined to make a name for herself on her own. And now she was here, ready to claim her place and he knew she would fight to the death for it. His Joya was a warrior. And he would really need to figure out a way to stop thinking of her as his. But how was he supposed to do that when everything in him wanted to possess her? To take her in his arms and show her that he'd never stopped wanting her?

"You were always much better than I was at not letting your passions get the best of you. But I've learned," she assured him.

He couldn't contain the caustic laugh that escaped him. "Except when it came to you. I always forgot myself when I was with you."

"You have a funny way of showing it, Rodrigo." Her eyes narrowed again, and she leaned in so their bodies were practically touching and he had to fist his hands to keep from bringing her against him.

"Is that a proposition, Esmeralda?" he taunted, pressing close enough to feel her heat.

That's when he saw it— right behind the frustration there was just a hint of desire in her eyes. He heard it in the way her breath hitched when he leaned into her. He felt it when her body reached for his even as she tried to keep some distance. When his eyes focused on her lush lips, they parted for him like he was the only water she'd seen after days in the desert. They were fools, both of them. Hadn't learned a thing in all these years, and yet he could not make himself walk away.

"Esmeralda." He said her name like it meant something all on its own. Because it did, *it always had.* He felt his pulse hammering in his chest, at once urgent and trepidatious. Once they'd done this, once this kiss happened, everything would change and Rodrigo could not bring himself to care.

He placed a hand on the back of her neck and brought her forward. "You make me crazy," he growled through gritted teeth, aching to close the last centimeter of distance between them.

"I hate that I want you this much," she muttered as her arms circled his neck.

Common sense was beyond him, need burning in him like a fever. "I could take you right here." The tension in the room pulsed around them as they stood there, poised to crash and burn before they'd even really started. The pressure of the door opening at his back sent him tumbling forward and almost knocked him on top of Esmeralda.

"Oh my goodness, I'm so sorry, Mr. Almanzar. I didn't realize anyone was here." He recognized the young woman as the executive assistant for one of the VPs. He couldn't quite remember which one, but it didn't matter. Hell, he should be thanking the woman for saving him from himself.

"That's fine. Miss Sambrano-Peña and I were just discussing some details about the five-year strategic plan." He glanced in Esme's direction and had to look away from the flush on her cheeks, because focusing on her obvious arousal would only lead to more bad decisions. "Can you give us a minute?"

The woman's eyes widened as she realized she'd interrupted something, but she quickly made a grab for the doorknob. "Of course."

The click of the door sounded like a gunshot in the quiet room, and he was sure he could hear the drumming of both their hearts. What a disaster.

"That can't happen again." Esmeralda's voice was low and husky, the heat of the past few minutes clearly still coursing through her veins. And right then, he wished he was the kind of man who could forget his responsibilities. But he was nothing if not dutiful. Hell, it was his need to always put his duty first that had cost him Esmeralda. Besides, it was all too far gone to fix any of it. This almost-kiss had been a desperate attempt to reclaim something that had long ago slipped from his fingers. The only way out was to move forward.

"It won't happen again." He looked at his watch. It was almost 7:00 p.m. and this day had been a decade. "I will show you to your office, and tomorrow first thing I will guide you through some of the material the board will want you to take into consideration."

Esmeralda nodded, but did not say a word for a long time. “I’m sure I’ll be fine. Just show me where I can work and I’ll take it from there.” She pulled the door open and stalked off.

He followed her out, feeling off-kilter and more than a little sexually frustrated. Whether she wanted it or not, he was going to do his job, and part of that was showing her how to do hers.

That was what he was known for after all, never deviating from the task at hand. Everything else could fall by the wayside, but Rodrigo Almanzar always delivered—even when it cost him his own happiness.

Five

"I'm only here to look through some of these files. It's easier than going back and forth. I'll be out of your hair in a minute."

Rodrigo stopped short when he found Esmeralda in his office with what looked like every single one of his programming binders sprawled over his meeting table. She'd arrived yesterday morning as if the previous day's boardroom blowout—and that almost-kiss—never happened and placidly asked for him to show her around. And as the board, and the whole world, expected him to, he did his job. He'd gotten her set up, and ever since they'd given each other a wide berth.

Well, physically at least, because so far, he hadn't

been able to go more than a minute without thinking about her. From where he stood in the doorway he could see she was looking through news clippings and show features from 2001, and had plastered sticky notes on a few others. It looked like she'd been at it for hours. It was barely 7:00 a.m.

"How long have you been here?" He looked at her again and noticed she was wearing different clothes than yesterday, so she must've gone home. Today she had on a pencil skirt in a deep burgundy and a heather-gray blouse. Her Gucci stilettos were off her feet and toppled over on the floor next to her. Her hair was in a top bun, smoothed back with her baby hair feathered out. He smiled when he saw the gold hoops in her ear. A Washington Heights girl through and through. Rodrigo thought to himself that Esmeralda would be good for this company, even if it was not as CEO.

"Mmm, maybe a bit over an hour," she said distractedly, as if that didn't mean she'd arrived literally at dawn. She looked up from the notes she was jotting down and took him in. Her face was bare, no makeup except for a little bit of lip gloss. She looked fresh and young, and so damn beautiful. Always so beautiful…and intense.

"There's so much to go over. I still don't have a full sense of what I'm going to do for the presentation, and the clock is ticking." She pointed at him, but the hostility wasn't there anymore, or at least it wasn't there now. "I meant what I said, Rodrigo. I'm fighting for it."

He shook his head, noticing the small smile tugging at her lips and he wished everything in him didn't react to her every word as deeply as it did. "I never expected for you to not give me a fight."

He had to watch himself very carefully with Esmeralda, because cordial was all well and good, but he could not even for a moment give her the impression this wasn't a fight to the death. "I enjoy a good competition. Here," he said, lifting up the bag in his hand. "I brought you something."

She eyed the bag suspiciously but when she saw the logo, a grin immediately appeared on her face. "You went to La Nueva?" she asked as he walked over to the table and placed the parcel in front of her on the table.

"It's in my neighborhood."

She gave him a suspicious look as she glanced at the contents. "You got me the cream cheese and guayaba Danish. How did you remember?" She sounded almost affronted he still knew what her favorite pastry was from the bakery they'd gone to as kids.

"You never ordered anything else in the thousand times we went there." Esmeralda may have forgotten that they had been in each other's lives from day one, but he never would. They were tied to each other and always would be. Their mothers had been best friends, but it had always been more than that. Hell, in those days where everything seemed to be falling apart after his father had lost everything to gambling, Ivelisse had been the one to help his mother pick up the pieces.

It had always seemed so wrong to him that Esmeralda could never be a part of Patricio's life. She lived in a small apartment and went to the neighborhood Catholic school, while her half-siblings lived in a Park Avenue penthouse and went to boarding school in Switzerland. Although for the most part that meant she was untouched by all the Sambrano drama, protected by a mother who could clearly see how that world could taint her daughter. And here she was now, a determined, strong woman, still blowing him away with that fire of hers. And he hoped that the tough exterior matched what was inside, because he would crush her hopes for that CEO position. There was no other option.

"We didn't go a thousand times," she muttered through a mouthful of pastry. He'd always enjoyed watching her eat. Esmeralda was not dainty or shy about what she loved. She took big bites and gulped things in—unapologetically ravenous for what brought her pleasure. There had been a time he'd been what pleased her the most, before he'd ruined everything with his need to do his duty despite who got hurt in the process. Before Patricio's refusal to see through Carmelina's lies.

He would never forget that day. He'd made up a story at work about scoping out some potential talent in LA and gotten on a Thursday-night redeye to spend three days with Esme. On Friday they'd driven out to Laguna Beach and eaten ceviche and drank cold beer in a restaurant on the water. Their Saturday plans to go to the Getty Villa had been completely ignored, and instead he'd kept her in bed until the afternoon. It had been all the more perfect because those moments were just theirs. They'd kept their relationship secret, because they'd both known that once their families knew it would be out of their hands. But he'd been hopeful in those few days, and foolish enough to think that the love they had for each other could endure anything. He had been so wrong.

On the Sunday morning his mother's plea for help on behalf of Ivelisse Peña shattered the joy of those few days. Gloria had delivered the news in hushed tones over the phone, telling him that on Friday Esmeralda's mother had received a notice saying she had one week to vacate the apartment she lived in. All because Carmelina had gotten in Patricio's head and he'd decided to turn the mother of his firstborn on the street.

Without telling Esmeralda why—Ivelisse had begged him not to tell her daughter what was happening until she at least had a new place to live—he'd jumped on a plane back to New York to intercede with Patricio. He'd found the man in his office, drunk off his head raving about paternity tests and Ivelisse being a liar. When Rodrigo finally got him sobered up enough to explain, Patricio showed him the "test"

Carmelina had produced as evidence that Esmeralda was not his child.

Knowing Carmelina, Rodrigo had made quick work of discovering that his mentor's wife had fabricated the whole thing. He'd tried to call the laboratory that supposedly had done it, and confirmed the place didn't exist. But the damage was already done and it was twofold, because as Rodrigo worked to help Ivelisse, the truth about the nature of his relationship with Patricio's daughter came to light. And so did the price he'd have to pay to make sure Esmeralda never found out the real reason her father had forced Ivelisse out of their home.

Rodrigo had risked his job, his mother's treatment and Patricio's help getting the Almanzar family out of the debt his father had sunk them into. Once his mentor figured out he was in love with Esme, Patricio demanded that Rodrigo end it. The older man had been furious, flying into a rage about Rodrigo keeping things from him, of going behind his back.

Rodrigo had taken all the insults and humiliation; he'd had no choice. But before he fell on the sword Patricio set for him, he asked for one last thing. One final guarantee that Carmelina could never attempt to do what she'd done again, then he gave Esmeralda up.

If it had only been him, he would've walked away from everything to be able to keep her. But he couldn't do it then, and he certainly could not now.

At least he'd protected her from Carmelina's vicious schemes and saved his own family.

Ten years later, knowing all the pain they'd both endured, he wondered if it had all been worth it.

"I didn't know you'd moved back Uptown." Esmeralda's voice brought Rodrigo back from his distressing trip down memory lane.

"I bought a brownstone in Sugar Hill a couple of years ago," he said as he sipped his café con leche and watched her eat. She gave him a wry look as she chewed like she couldn't quite figure out why he'd done that. Seven years ago, right after he'd taken the position of chief content officer for Sambrano, he'd bought himself an obnoxious condo in a building downtown. He'd gotten it because it seemed like the kind of place that successful people in movies about New York City seemed to live in, but it never fit him. When his mother's illness came back a couple years earlier he made the move so he could be closer to her. "It's nice to be back in the old neighborhood."

She looked at him suspiciously, still picking at her Danish. "You're only like ten blocks from Mami and me."

He wasn't sure if it was a statement of fact or a rebuke, but for the sake of his own sanity, he decided to veer off the subject of their parents and their history. It was pure survival instinct at this point. He pulled a chair from the table she was sitting at, far enough away that he wouldn't be tempted to reach over and clean the crumbs of pastry that were adorably stuck to the side of her mouth.

"Did you see Octavio's invitation for the reception tonight?" he asked, leaning back on the chair, his eyes still stuck on her mouth as her tongue lapped at the crumbs. It would be a miracle if he managed to keep his head this week. Everything about this woman was appealing. His eyes roamed over her body; her ample bosom looked downright sinful in that tailored blouse that was unbuttoned far enough he could see the plunge of her breasts. Through the fabric he caught a glimpse of the lace of her bra, and he had to cross his legs to keep from embarrassing himself.

"Eyes on my face, Rodrigo."

I'm trying, Esmeralda, but when you lick your lips like that my eyes just start roaming on their own.

The teasing tone in her voice made his face flush with heat, but how could he not stare at the embodiment of his every desire sitting only a few feet away?

"And yes, I saw the invitation. I'm not going."

Her dismissive tone annoyed Rodrigo. He could deal with pissed Esmeralda, but petulance was never something he could handle well. "It's not a suggestion. You *have* to go, Esmeralda. All of our biggest advertisers will be there." She shook her head stubbornly as he spoke and he couldn't decide if he wanted to throttle her or kiss some sense into her.

"I don't have anything suitable to wear to a formal reception at The Cloisters, Rodrigo!" Her eyes widened at the mention of the museum of medieval art in upper Manhattan where the event would take place. He could understand her feeling intimidated—as far as gala locations went, that one was definitely for the New York City A-listers crowd.

"Tantrums are not going to help you this week, Joya." He almost laughed at the way her eyes narrowed, the Danish halfway to her mouth. But treating her with kid gloves was not going to help either of them. "Take this as the good faith advice that it is. It's not a smart move for you to miss this chance to interact with the board. It will be good for them to see how you handle yourself, how you could potentially represent the studio. You're a shareholder now and that won't change even if you're not CEO."

She opened her mouth, about to protest, but he held up his palm. "This isn't about us being competitors, it's about you assuming your place as part of the Sambrano family. You need to think of the big picture, Esmeralda. You now own a quarter of a billion-dollar company. This isn't you trying to get a job on a set or to get someone to look at your pilot. This is the big leagues, and you need to start acting like you get that." She was still glaring at him, but he could see the set of her shoulders had drooped ever so slightly. "I'm giving you good advice. Take it."

She took another sip from her mug, which from the smell wafting toward him seemed to be something spicy and aromatic—maybe Masala chai. She'd always loved that. She was staring into space, processing what he'd told her. He could see the precise moment she saw the value of his words. She was smart, smarter than any of the fools running around the building. And she'd always deserved a seat at the table.

Too bad that the seat she wanted was one he was not ready to give up. When she turned her eyes to him they were slightly less contentious.

"I see your point, but I really don't have anything to wear." She lifted a shoulder as she ran a finger over the edges of the binder in front of her. "I get that people didn't have a chance to let me know it was happening since I only showed up the day before yesterday, so it's not that I'm mad or anything. I just don't have the time to spend the entire day hunting for a designer gown."

"Leave it to me." It was out of his mouth before he could stop himself. "I'll find you a gown and you focus on your work until it's time to get ready." He could see it already. Something satiny and expensive that hugged her every curve.

"Suit yourself. I'm certainly not going shopping like a Dominican Cinderella when I have barely five days to come up with a whole strategic vision for the studio. This is no time to play games."

He laughed and she scowled. "I assure you, none of this is a game. And no one is getting a fairy-tale ending." Esmeralda wasn't sure why Rodrigo would say that, but she wasn't going to let his tough love act get in her head.

She had no intention of going to a reception or anywhere else with him. No matter how delicious he looked in the navy suit he had on. The man had no right to look that good at 7:00 a.m., especially in a blue-and-yellow shirt. The audacity. Who could even pull off that color combination? Rodrigo, that's who.

She'd almost kissed him. Ten years of telling herself she wanted nothing to do with him. That she despised him for betraying her. That if she ever saw him again she would tell him all the ways he'd hurt her. And it had literally taken *seconds* alone with him to have her swooning at his feet. Yeah, this man was not good for her, and what she needed was to pick up all the binders she'd pulled off his shelves and go to her office across the hall.

Instead she stared at him as he sipped his coffee. "Do you still take it teeth-rottingly sweet?" What in the world? Why did she ask him that? Was she trying to *flirt* with the man?

He winked at her. The bastard. His big body was sprawled on an office chair that frankly looked a bit spindly to accommodate all that Cuban–Puerto Rican real estate. He was a beautiful man. No question about it. Brown skin, dark eyes fringed with eyelashes most women would kill for, and a broad mouth with full, fleshy lips that she could still remember on her skin.

Focus, Esmeralda. FOCUS.

The presentation. That was what she was supposed to be talking to Rodrigo about, not fixating on how his hands had gripped her two nights ago. Her belly did a somersault at the thought of how close she'd come to kissing him, and everything that moment had brought roaring back. Taking in a shaky breath, Esme willed herself to redirect her focus. Rodrigo was supposed to help her, so she could ask him some questions. Hell, she needed to.

Yesterday she'd taken the day to review some of the material she'd been given, and she had a sense of what direction she wanted to go with her presentation, but there were a few things that weren't adding up. She needed some institutional knowledge, some insight, and the only person she could get it from was Rodrigo.

"Can I ask you something?" He dipped his head in response, so she sat up. "Where did all the Afro-Latinx people go?"

He straightened in the chair as soon as she posed the question, throwing his shoulders back for good measure. It was almost like he was readying himself for them to have it out. She knew he got what she was asking, but was curious to hear what excuses he'd make. His brows dipped and the line of his mouth hardened at whatever he was thinking about.

Sambrano had begun as a studio that produced content for *all* Latinx communities. While the Spanish-language networks that came later focused on catering to a very specific kind of audience, Sambrano always embraced the many shades and sides to Latinx identity. They celebrated the Black and Indigenous communities that also wanted to see themselves reflected positively on screen, when every other outlet seemed content with erasing them. No surprise there since her father was a Black man, and for Patricio, celebrating his heritage had seemed—at least in the beginning—to be a vital part of the Sambrano brand.

In the '90s the studio had embraced the same idea as other American networks who were producing hit shows with all-Black casts. Other Spanish-language networks refused to cast Black and Indigenous casts and production staff, while Sambrano made them a central part of their programming. It had made the studio stand out to Latinx audiences, but somewhere in the past twenty years that had fallen by the wayside. Looking at the movies and TV shows Sambrano was currently producing, it seemed like they'd forgotten their roots, and Esmeralda couldn't figure out why they'd made that change. She did notice the programming had gotten a bit more diverse since Rodrigo had been chief content officer, but even with those efforts it was not even a shadow of what it had been at the start. She wanted to know why her father, who had seemed almost fervently committed to represent every face of the Latinx community, had betrayed his own vision.

Rodrigo considered her for a minute before he

opened his mouth. "Depending on who you ask you will get different answers to that question."

"I want to hear *your* answer." Esmeralda didn't know too many things about who Rodrigo had become in these past ten years, but she knew there was no one more devoted to the studio than him.

He shifted in his chair again, his body tense now. He clearly wasn't sure how to answer this without pointing fingers. He wouldn't like doing that. Always the quintessential company man.

"Carmelina always had a bigger influence on Patricio than was advisable. He was a proud man, but his insecurities about his lack of education would get to him. And Carmelina knew how to prey on them. She would flaunt her Ivy League degree, her family's pedigree, and he'd end up taking her advice, even to his own detriment. That's how it started, anyway." Rodrigo shook his head distastefully at whatever he was remembering. "She always had a million ideas." He smiled then, but it was sharp, cold. "And most of them involved making Sambrano a carbon copy of American networks, to take all the Latinx culture out of it and just have the same type of programming but in Spanish." There was something in his expression, a barely restrained frustration that told her this was something he'd been seething about for a long time. "I always pushed back, reminding Patricio the core values of the studio were to make movies and television our people could see themselves in. But

Carmelina was relentless. She never understood that our biggest asset was leaning into our authenticity."

Bitterness filled Esme's mouth. How had her father let Carmelina destroy his legacy? How had Rodrigo let that happen?

"Aren't you the chief content officer? How did you let her influence things so much?" She sounded judgmental, and she knew criticizing the man would probably not help matters. But she was annoyed at all this. Annoyed that her father had gone along with his wife's greedy intentions, annoyed that she had been kept out, annoyed that Rodrigo seemed to always let people's shitty behavior slide if it meant he got to keep his multi-million-dollar salary. Yeah… she'd seen the payroll and her eyes were still watering at the figures she saw.

He gave her a long, assessing look, clearly considering what to say. "I bet it's nice to stroll in and start making judgments, but you don't know what it's been like. I'm not Onyx or Perla, or even you. I don't have 'Sambrano' attached to my name. Your father lost sight of his mission, but the man could never admit he was wrong. And that meant the rest of us could only mitigate the damage and hope he eventually saw the error of his ways. Then he got sick." With every word she could see his shoulders stiffen and his jaw tick with tension. Barely restrained frustration blended with the grief written across his face.

"If it were up to Carmelina, this place wouldn't even be a shadow of what it used to be. The only reason there's anything left is because I've fought tooth and nail to save it. And don't think she hasn't tried to bully me into being her accomplice in schemes. But contrary to what the gossips will tell you, I'm not for sale." He stood up then, dropping the empty coffee cup in the wastebasket as he moved closer to her. "And that's one of the many reasons I should be in charge of this studio," he said, all traces of the amiable conversation they'd been having completely gone. "You have no idea what you're up against, Esmeralda. This is a fight for the future of this company, and if you think I'll back down just because you're involved, then you don't know me at all."

"Oh, believe me, I'm counting on getting stabbed in the back by you."

He reared back like she'd slapped him in the face, but he recovered quickly, and soon he was leaning in across the table, face twisted in anger. "Unlike Patricio's wife and his children, I care about what happens to this place. Or maybe now that you have your shares you want to make sure to get your dividends..."

That was a low blow, but it was a good reminder that Rodrigo was not on her side. "I've never counted on a cent from Patricio Sambrano," she said, standing up to her full height. If he wanted to fight dirty and say hurtful things then she had ten years' worth of grievances to hurl at Rodrigo Almanzar. "You of all people should know that. Because if I recall correctly, you had a first-row seat to my father putting my mother out on the street on a whim. Or did you block that out of your memory together with every other thing about me you seem to have erased?"

His nostrils flared at that and she knew her words had struck true. His light brown skin flushed with red. Yeah, he *should* be ashamed of himself.

"You were the one who cut off all contact, Esmeralda," he said through gritted teeth. "I never said we couldn't be friends. Yo nunca—"

She could see the hurt in his eyes and immediately the urge to back down rose in her. But she smothered it out. She was tired of being overlooked, of being ignored. Of the men in her life walking out on her and then expecting her to run back and forgive them. And now she was right back there, to that nightmare of a weekend.

"You would never what?" The trip had been almost a year in the making. Rodrigo had tried and failed to get out of work for months, until he finally got a few days off to come and see her. She'd been in love and sure they were starting something that could last forever, but she'd been mistaken of course. She'd been foolish about everything when it came to this man. "You would never tell me you loved me, sleep with me, only to ghost me the next morning? Or betray me for power and money? Oh, wait," she said dramatically, then pointed a finger at him. "That's exactly what you did."

His face seemed to turn to stone and her chest ached from what she was doing. She felt wretched, and yet she could not seem to stop herself. It was as if she'd had this poison sitting in her gut for ten years and now that it had started coming out she had to purge all of it.

"My father hurt me and abandoned me, but I never expected any better from him. You? You tore my heart out."

She walked out before he could respond and before he could see the tears that were rolling down her face. And as she reached her office she wondered how much of herself she was willing to lose in order to win this game.

Six

"What is this supposed to be?"

Rodrigo was still stewing over their earlier conversation—argument, fight, whatever. So Esmeralda appearing in his office looking pissed and pushing a clothing rack full of evening dresses only sank his mood further.

"It's a selection of dresses for you to pick from for the reception tonight." He didn't look up from the email he was sending off.

One more investor who had appeared out of nowhere wanting to acquire the studio. This had Carmelina's fingerprints all over it. The woman was nothing if not persistent. From the moment they'd heard about Patricio's will she'd been trying to get him on her side. That really would be a deal with the devil.

"I said I was not going," Esmeralda growled.

He kept typing. "There is also a makeup artist available if you need it." When he finally looked up, he found her fuming by his desk. "Did Marquito bring the shoes?" Rodrigo asked, ignoring her searing glare.

Her jaw actually dropped at that last part, and he would've laughed if she didn't look like she could murder him. "That's what that big box was? Wait, Marquito's here?"

He wished his chest didn't light up like the Rockefeller Center Christmas tree at the affection in Esmeralda's voice at the mention of his younger brother. Marcos was a sought-after celebrity stylist and at twenty-eight was making a name for himself in the industry. Rodrigo had asked for his help only a couple of hours ago and it seemed he'd delivered.

"Did I get the wrong size?" He doubted it. When it came to Esmeralda's body, every curve and every angle was forever etched in his memory. "Marquito's not here. He sent the dresses by messenger."

"Oh." She looked genuinely disappointed. She'd always been kind to his little brother and when Marcos had been a ball of teen angst and confusion she'd been the first person he'd come out to. Rodrigo would always be grateful to her for that, but that was neither here nor there at the moment.

"Are you listening to me, Rodrigo?" The exasperation in her voice brought him out of his thoughts. He kept going into his head. Distraction was not his friend. Not this week.

"Sorry," he muttered, as he turned back to her. "Is there a problem with the dresses?"

"No, they're perfect, which only makes this that much more irritating."

"Okay, so what's the problem then?" he asked gruffly, feeling unsettled with this woman in his space.

She threw her arms up and came closer to the desk. Her mouth pursed in an adorably irritated expression and he once again had to remind himself his instinct to reach out to her was not just stupid, it was self-destructive. No matter what happened this week there would be a falling-out. If she got the job, he knew he'd be crushed. If he got it, that would only give her another reason to hate him.

"Listen, I appreciate you trying to give me my very own *Pretty Woman* moment this week, but I already said I'm not going to this party." He dearly wished that his traitorous cock didn't pulse at that sexy huskiness of her voice. "It's not worth losing an entire evening mingling and drinking champagne when I could be working." She had both hands on her hips, her face flushed, and he wondered if this proximity was getting to her, too.

But before he could even open his mouth, the last person he wanted to see walked into his office, as if he'd conjured her up with his thoughts.

"Isn't this cozy? Rodrigo, are you spending the company's money on dresses now? I thought that big salary we paid you was to actually do work." Carmelina Sambrano knew less about television and moviemaking than a kindergartener, and yet she fancied herself an expert on what his job entailed. He was surprised it had taken this long for her to come and harass Esme.

He looked over at the younger woman and saw that she was looking at her father's widow through narrowed eyes. There was no love lost there, and that was with Esmeralda unaware of just how low Carmelina had gone to try to push her out. And as far as he was concerned she would never know. He'd promised Ivelisse he'd never tell and he didn't plan to go back on his word.

But now Esme was poised to take possession of the prize Patricio's widow had spent decades scheming to control. Carmelina wasn't stupid, but she was getting more desperate by the day. And a desperate Carmelina was very dangerous.

"What do you want?" He didn't even attempt to mask his derision for her.

Carmelina was dressed in her usual matching jacket and skirt combo, evoking old-school Jackie O. It was probably custom Chanel. But it didn't matter how much money the woman spent on designer clothes, she made everything look cheap.

"Just came to personally let you know I've forbidden any private footage of my husband from being used for this farce." She turned to Esme then. "If you don't know anything about your father, it's because he wanted it that way. You're going to have to continue your little attempt at moneygrubbing without watching his interviews."

"Carmelina," Rodrigo snapped, menace clear in his voice. "Watch your tone."

But Esmeralda didn't flinch or give any indication she was fazed by the woman's vitriol. "I never requested any footage," she said, indifferent. "I have plenty to work with."

"*I* asked that the footage be made available to you," Rodrigo retorted. "It's from a documentary we were planning as part of the studio's thirty-fifth anniversary next year. But we weren't able to finish it." That pang of dull pain he still felt whenever he thought about Patricio flared in his chest as he spoke to Esme. He could see the conflicted sadness in her eyes at the mention of her father's passing, such a contrast to Carmelina's dismissive scoff.

"Is he being very helpful, giving you guidance and advice?" The bitterness that fueled Carmelina resonated in every word she said. "The honorable Rodrigo Almanzar, who turned his back on his own family so he could steal my son's rightful place. Don't trust him, querida. This one would betray his own mother to keep this office." Her voice dripped with contempt, but he'd learned long ago to not let Carmelina's words get to him. The only thing he cared about was that she didn't get her talons into Esmeralda. *That* he would not tolerate.

Carmelina wasn't finished. "He's the one you need to be careful with, you know. I don't need Sambrano." She smiled sharply, a hyena with her prey in her sights. "I have *never* needed Sambrano Studios—Patricio married *me* for *my* money." She laughed shrilly. "I'm doing this to preserve my husband's legacy and what rightfully belongs to his *legitimate* children."

He would never lay a hand on a woman, and that was the only thing that kept him from physically removing Patricio's widow from his office.

"Carmelina, get out," he snarled, fury boiling over in an instant. The things he could throw in her face about the messes he'd had to get her son out of through the years…

"I have a right to Sambrano, too," Esmeralda said calmly, as if Carmelina's hateful words had barely registered.

"Leave." Even he could hear the menace in his voice.

The older woman shrugged, an unfriendly smile on her lips. "So testy. Don't worry. I'm going." She made for the door, but stopped again in front of the rack of dresses. "There's not couture expensive enough to hide the fact that you're Patricio's bastard."

Esmeralda took her hand off the rack and moved until she was just a few feet away from Carmelina, the smile on her lips dangerous and cold in a way he'd never seen from her.

"Well then," she said, feigning a placidness she was clearly not feeling. "If people are wagging their tongues anyway I might as well make an appearance at the reception." Esme crossed her arms and looked straight at her father's widow. "And if you think coming over here to call me names is going to distract me from wanting to take all this from you, you have another thing coming. Now, if you'll excuse me, I have dresses to try on."

"Esmeralda, stay right where you are," he demanded, making the younger woman stop in her tracks. "Carmelina, if you're done. Miss Sambrano-Peña and I have things to discuss."

"You're not winning this," Carmelina warned Esmeralda before storming out. Rodrigo's heart pounded like a drum in his chest. But it had nothing to do with Carmelina and everything to do with the hellion in front of him. Esmeralda. Time and distance had done nothing to diminish his desire for her. And now, seeing her like this, standing up proudly, unashamed. Ready to claim her place. It cracked something in him. Despite the mess he'd made of things, he was proud of her, admired her strength.

"She's really still that terrible, isn't she?" Esme asked shakily, after he closed the door to the office. She'd held her own but he could see Carmelina had gotten to her.

"She's worse," he assured her, exhausted from the

exchange. “Forget her. Despite what Carmelina may think, she has no power to override the board’s decisions. You and I are still in the running for CEO and she only gets one vote in that decision.”

“More like three if you count my siblings,” she said with distaste, and he couldn’t deny that was probably true. Perla and Onyx could care less if the studio went up in flames as long as someone still covered their Amex bills.

“My hope is that it won’t come down to their three votes. Carmelina has a lot of enemies on that board, and people won’t just go along with her. Put her out of your mind for now. I have something to show you.” He lifted his hand to take hers, but then just let it fall to his side, curbing once more the almost overwhelming need to touch her. He went to the hidden door on the wall parallel to his desk and pushed on the panel. It slid to the side to reveal the hidden bedroom suite that Patricio had built for himself. Rodrigo had no idea why he was doing this. There was no reason for him to show her this now.

“You’re joking,” Esme said, as she looked at the narrow hallway that led to a spacious bedroom with an en suite bathroom. “Please tell me this isn’t some kind of assignation room, because I really don’t think I can handle that image of my father.”

A laugh burst out of him at the feigned horror in her voice, and the warmth that spread in his chest at being able to hear her make jokes again was a revelation. “I can’t confirm or deny what went on in this room, but I do know that Patricio had it built a long time ago. The man always had a flair for imitating some of the telenovelas he produced, for better or worse." He frowned at the memory of the night his mentor had first shown him what was behind the secret panel. Patricio had confessed that not even six months into their marriage, he'd needed to find a way to get some distance from Carmelina. He lived for his work, so he'd built himself a suite where he could stay when he needed to focus on Sambrano.

"His marriage to Carmelina was never a happy one. It was a business arrangement that those two had, and initially I imagine it seemed mutually beneficial, but in the last ten years I saw Patricio become harder…bitter. They brought out the worst in each other. He always said that the only person who could remind him of who he was before he built all this was your mother."

"He didn't deserve her," she said quietly, still not taking a step toward the bedroom.

"No, he didn't. And I think how things ended with them was one of his biggest regrets." He extended a hand toward the bedroom. "You can change in there. Figure out which dress you want to wear." He pointed at the garment bag hanging from a hook on the wall next to his office door. "I'm changing here, too."

She didn't look too sure about it, but when he pushed the rack into the room she followed. "My assistant can get you that makeup artist."

This time her expression was hard to decipher.

Not shuttered, but also not exactly open, either. "I think I can handle my hair and makeup." She paused as she looked at him again, like she was hoping to find whatever underlying motives he had to do this for her. "But thank you for the dress. I think you're right. I need to show the board *and* Carmelina that I'm not planning on scurrying away. I'm here to work, but I'm also here to claim my place. And if that means champagne and canapés at The Cloisters, then so be it."

With that she pushed the rack the rest of the way into the suite and closed the door behind it. Rodrigo assumed she'd go back to her office until it was time to get ready. But instead she leaned against the door and turned her face up to look at him. There was something in her eyes he couldn't quite read. "Why are you being nice to me?"

And that was the two-hundred-million-dollar question, wasn't it? He could say all kinds of things, that he owed it to Patricio, that he was a professional and he would give anyone else the same courtesy, but those would all be lies. The truth felt like a dagger on his tongue, sharp and deadly.

"I'm nice to everyone," he lied.

"You're so full of it." The sly smile on her face smoothed the edges in her words. God he wanted her. The need to press her to him was a tangible force in the air. But if there was a time to live up to his supposed stoicism, it was now. He stepped away and went back to his desk.

"Let me know when you need the room to change, and I'll make sure to give you space," he said gruffly, avoiding her gaze.

"Right," she said, heading for the door. She sounded as flustered as he felt. "I need to get a few things done, before I start getting ready. Could you check the mock-up I sent you? I'd like to start working on my concept tonight. Just because I'm taking a few hours to participate in this rich people show-and-tell doesn't mean I'm not coming back here to work after."

He nodded as the door slid closed behind her. Nobody needed to know that his eyes were riveted to the glorious view of her perfect ass as she walked away. He was in over his head. A lifetime of doggedly working after a singular goal was threatening to slip away. All because the one person he could see himself giving everything up for was the one standing between him and his dream.

Seven

"Dammit." Esmeralda let out another frustrated sigh as she tried and failed to zip up her dress. It was so bizarre to be in this room. A place her father escaped to when things were not going well in his home life. This was a level of intimacy she'd never had with him when he was alive. On the tall dresser—which she supposed had stored changes of clothes and personal things—were some framed photographs. Some of her. That had surprised her. One was from her second birthday—her parents on either side of her, strained smiles on their faces. She didn't remember it, but she knew in those first few years Patricio had made appearances for special occasions. There was another photo from her high school graduation. And the most recent one of her receiving an award for a short film she'd presented at the Tribeca Film Festival.

It had pierced something in her to see she'd had a place among his other children. That the picture of her and her mother was there with the rest of them. That he hadn't forgotten her, even though it had always felt that to her father she'd never existed. She'd always looked in from outside when it came to his life. And now here she was in his inner sanctum, only to realize he'd kept reminders of her around. She had no idea what to do with any of it, and worse, the only person she wanted to talk about it with was the last man she needed to be around when she was feeling this messy. Damn Rodrigo for standing up for her today. For getting her gorgeous dresses that fit her perfectly. For his sinful mouth and swoon-worthy shoulders, and most of all for making her feel this raw again.

"Ugh, crying is not the move right now," she said, frustrated as she blinked, trying to keep the tears that were threatening to escape from ruining her perfect smoky eye. And still she could not zip up her dress. She looked at the alarm clock next to the bed and saw that it was almost six. Okay, screw it, she was going to need his help with this dress. She made her way to the sliding door that led into the CEO office and opened it slowly.

Rodrigo was standing with his back to her, on the other side of the room, looking out of the enormous windows that provided a heart-stopping view of a June Manhattan sunset. He did cut a dashing figure in his suit. Everything had to be just so with Rodrigo Almanzar, everything in its place. But with her he'd been messy and free. Funny and passionate. For so many years he had meant so much to her—if she was honest with herself, he still did. But she could not walk away from this fight.

It would ruin things for them forever, she knew that. Rodrigo would feel betrayed. He'd resent her. And wasn't that what she'd said she wanted? A chance to get back at him? Well, her taking the CEO position from him would certainly accomplish that.

"Rodrigo," she said into the quiet room, and he turned. God, but the man was a sight standing in the warm glow of the golden hour. He could always trip her up with just a look. He kept his hair very short, and his face clean-shaven. Always so formal. Tonight's dark blue tuxedo made him look like a Tom Ford model. Her eyes glommed on to him as he walked over to her and she did not miss that his eyes were burning, too.

By the time he got to her the beating of her heart was so intense she could feel it in her throat. She felt naked. Bare to him in too many ways that felt utterly dangerous. So she hid from him. She turned around and walked back into her father's secret bedroom, feeling too exposed to be in the office where anyone could see. He followed her in without a word, and she did not dare turn around. Finally, when she got to the front of the bed, she asked the question without looking up. "Can you zip me up?"

"You picked the green one," he said huskily. She'd settled on an emerald green A-line sleeveless dress by Christian Siriano. One of her goals in life had been to wear one of his creations, and even though this whole situation would probably end up blowing up in her face, she could at least have this memory.

Although now that she was the owner of a quarter of Sambrano, she supposed there could be more Siriano in her future…

She heard the quick intake of breath and felt the heat of him as he came even closer. "This color is perfect on you, Joya." There was that name again. The one she'd always told herself—and him—she hated but melted for whenever he uttered it.

He gripped her waist as his other hand traced the bare skin of her back with a finger that could've been flames licking at her skin. She didn't protest, she didn't move away, entranced by the feel of him. She'd told herself so many times this man meant nothing her. And yet just a brush of his fingers had her ready to toss out the window every self-protective instinct she had. She wanted to lean in, take those strong hands and wrap them around her waist. Let her head fall on his shoulder; but he only zipped her dress, and stepped back.

"Turn around, I want to see you."

She should be annoyed at his demanding tone. She should tell him to get out of the room, that she didn't need him anymore. She should guard her heart from someone who could so easily trample it. But instead, she turned her bare feet on the plush carpet to face him. And what she found in his eyes could easily raze them both down to ashes.

"Hermosa, mi Joya." His voice was rough with desire, and she knew in that moment, whatever he asked for she'd give him. He pressed closer, so she had to tip her head to look at his face. "Having you this close and not being able to touch you is hell." His voice was gravel and smoke as he brushed his knuckles against her cheek. She closed her eyes at the contact, her breath hitching from the effect his closeness had on her. Always overwhelming. Like he was the only person in the world.

"I want to kiss you, Esmeralda." She shook her head at the statement, even as a frustrated little whine escaped her lips.

Her arms were already circling around his neck. "If we're going to do this, just do it, Rodrigo." Without hesitation he crushed her mouth with his and the world fell away. His tongue stole in, and it was like not a single day had passed since they'd last done this. She pressed herself to him as he peppered her neck with fluttering kisses. Somewhere in the back of her mind she knew this was the height of stupidity, that they were both playing with fire. That if anyone found about this, she would probably sink her chances to get approved by the board. But it was so hard to think when he was whispering intoxicatingly delicious things in Spanish. Preciosa, amada…mia.

It was madness for him to call her his, and what was worse, she reveled in it. She wanted it so desperately that her skin prickled, her body tightening and loosening under his skilled touch.

"I can't get enough of you. I never could." He sounded bewildered. Like he couldn't quite figure out how it was that he'd gotten there.

That made two of them.

Esmeralda knew they should stop. They were supposed to head to the party soon and she'd for sure have to refresh her makeup now that she'd decided to throw all her boundaries out the window. But instead of stopping she threw her head back and let him make his way down her neck, his teeth grazing her skin as he tightened one hand on her backside and the other pulled down the strap of her dress. "Can I kiss you here?" he asked as his breath feathered over her breasts.

"Yes." She was on an express bus to Bad Decision Central and she could not be bothered to stop. He grazed his lips over her skin until he brushed the edge of the gown and flicked his tongue over her sensitive skin. She was breathless from the pleasure of it. She pressed a hand to the apex of her thighs, aching for him.

"You drive me crazy," he growled as he crushed her to him, his arousal like a fire iron against her belly. Her mouth watered at the thought of taking him in her mouth. She was about to tell him so. But shc must havc had some sensible angels watching over her, because right when she'd been about to burn through the last of her senses, a female voice calling for Rodrigo kept her from ruining everything.

Eight

"*Ex*-girlfriend," Rodrigo reminded Esmeralda for the fifth time since they'd arrived at The Cloisters. He should've been glad that his ex, Jimena, had shown up when she did. Saving him from himself and the utterly idiotic thing he'd been about to do. He didn't know what was going on with him. Ever since Esmeralda has stepped into that boardroom he'd been doing one stupid thing after the other. And what was worse, he could not make himself feel sorry for any of it. And didn't that make him a fool.

"She certainly seemed all cozy with you for being an ex." He returned his attention to Esmeralda, who was currently glaring at the beautifully lit courtyard where the reception was being hosted. The Cloisters were built as a replica of a medieval French abbey, with priceless tapestries and grand limestone arches everywhere. The reception was in a semi-enclosed rose garden, which was lit by what seemed like thousands of twinkling lights. It was stunning, but so far Esmeralda seemed unimpressed. She'd been in a mood on the drive over to the reception, too, as if he'd violated some kind of code by dating someone without her knowledge.

No. That primal thing pulsing in his chest was not satisfaction from seeing her jealous. Because he was not that stupid. Except, Esmeralda had always been the one place where Rodrigo forgot himself. The person who drove him to break his carefully guarded rules. She'd been the one person in his life who could always recognize the toll it took on him to hold his family together when his father lost everything they had in casinos. She had been the one to show up at the hospital while he waited for his mother to have her first round of chemo that summer they'd become more than friends. She'd been his harbor, and he'd desperately wanted to be hers. But instead he'd been one more person in her life to disappoint her.

"We're friends, Esmeralda."

She pursed her lips in a familiar expression he recognized as "stop BSing me" and his lips tugged up of their own volition. "We're grown adults who had a relationship, and then when things ran their course, we ended it amicably." He shrugged while she scowled and no matter what he did that feeling like his chest was expanding would not quit. Yes, he liked that she was being possessive. Even if he could do absolutely nothing with that.

"We're colleagues. She's one of the legal counsels for Sambrano, and honestly we're better as friends." Esme raised an eyebrow in question, apparently still too annoyed at him to talk. He couldn't help the humor in his voice when he explained. "It means we're both too committed to our jobs to be good partners."

"So you say."

Damn, but she was sexy when she got like this. He dearly wished he could drag her to a dark corner and give her a real reason to be hot and bothered. Could she really be upset about this? Or maybe Jimena said something to her. The woman could be a bit of a pit bull when it came to her loved ones, and Esme *was* technically gunning for his job. "Did she say anything untoward to you when I excused myself to use the restroom?"

He cleared his throat at the mention of the moment after Jimena had walked in on them kissing. He'd had to escape to another room before he embarrassed himself.

To his relief Esme shook her head. "No. Nothing like that. She wasn't super friendly, but she wasn't hostile, either. I didn't know that was your type," she said, before taking a sip from the flute of Moët she'd gotten off one of the servers. Again his dick was getting ideas. But it was hard not to when she was looking at him with those curious tawny eyes, her sensual mouth parted slightly as if she was waiting for his answer with bated breath.

"My type?" he asked tersely, and that brought a pink flush to her skin, and damn but he wanted to ravage her.

"Ivy League prep school, Latinx dynasty." He tried to read her expression, listened for mockery in her tone. To his surprise all he caught was a bit of discomfort there. She looked…embarrassed as her gaze roamed the crowded room. "We've been here less than ten minutes and you've already run into three people you went to Yale with." Ah, she felt out of place. Esmeralda hated feeling like an outsider. She always had. And if she'd been his, he'd make sure every person in this room knew she was a queen. That they needed to bow down to her. It was what she deserved. But she wasn't his anything. Not anymore.

"You mean pretentious asses who think they're better than everyone?" His teasing tonc brought a smile to her lips.

"Yeah. Something like that." She smiled wide and again a pulse of something that felt a lot like happiness glowed in his chest. And he absolutely needed to wean himself off the need to comfort Esmeralda. Him trying to fulfill that particular role had already cost him too much.

"It's the world you're fighting to get into. Don't

lose sight of that," he answered harshly and he saw the moment his words sank in. The softness in her mouth turned into a taut line and her honey-colored eyes, which had been wide and curious seconds before, narrowed in a shuttered expression.

"Oh, believe me. I'm very aware of the kind of compromises involved. I've seen it happen." She ran her eyes over him and then stormed off without another word.

His face tightened and his pulse quickened as shame coursed through him—and he welcomed it. This was what needed to happen. Pushing her away was the sane thing to do. He would give her the help she needed like he'd been tasked. But nothing between them could be like it used to. Because there was no middle ground for him when it came to Esmeralda. And at the end of this week he would have to be ruthless if he wanted to stay CEO.

"She's seen the error of her ways then." Instead of answering Jimena's taunt he took a long drink from his tumbler of Zacapa Centenario as he watched Esme storm off.

"You're not funny. And is sneaking up on people your new hobby?" he asked gruffly as he turned to face his friend.

She grinned as she reached for his glass.

"Get your own, Jimena."

"Oh, my. So moody," she muttered, looking in the direction Esmeralda had gone. "She can clearly still get under your skin. And wow, you're on her like a hawk."

"I don't know what you're talking about." He sounded pissed off and distracted because he was, tracking every step his rival for the top job at the studio made around the courtyard. He noticed he wasn't the only person aware of the fact that Esmeralda Sambrano was the most stunning woman in the room. People were turning to look at her and, yes, it was curiosity, at least at first, but plenty of them were sending her appreciative and very long glances as she made her way through the crowd. Once she got to the bar, she was barely standing there for a second when men started swarming her. She was handling them like a pro, though. Polite but keeping her distance.

"I'm just making sure she's talking to the right people."

Jimena laughed at that, because he was lying his ass off and they both knew it. "*Sure*, you're all business. She's nice, not what I expected. But she's too pure, Rodrigo. She won't be able to swim with these sharks and keep that idealism."

"She can handle them. I wasn't sure she was up for it, but she's a fighter. You should've seen her today going toe to toe with Carmelina. People underestimate her because she's not cynical and jaded. She's not what they're used to. But she's sharp and she's hungry. She's willing to bust her ass to get what she wants and that's how she can win." He meant every word, too. He knew her father's rejection hurt her, but not growing up around the likes of Carmelina Sambrano and her scheming had let Esme grow in ways she would not have been able to otherwise. She had integrity and a work ethic like only the child of immigrants could have, and that would take her far.

"Sharp, hungry and willing to work is not exactly what I'd associate with Sambrano offspring, that's for sure." Jimena was not a fan of Carmelina *or* her children. The three of them had been an ongoing headache for the entire legal department at the studio. "I know you want this job, but are you willing to see her get destroyed by the likes of Carmelina Sambrano? Because that's what she'll do under the guise of 'protecting the legacy.' Try to break her down. She's done it before. She did it to Patricio." Jimena's voice was barely over a whisper when she said that last part. And she was right, Patricio's illness had ravaged him, but his wife had accelerated the process.

Rodrigo kept his gaze on Esmeralda as he talked to Jimena. "I'll make sure Carmelina doesn't get up to any of her tricks, but this is a competition and I'm not Esmeralda's protector."

That elicited an amused laugh from Jimena. "Are you sure about that?"

"I'm serious, I—"

He never got the last of that sentence out because at the next moment Onyx Sambrano made sure every pair of eyes in the place were on him and Esmeralda.

* * *

Esmeralda let her eyes roam around the room and noticed that Carmelina and Onyx were talking in a corner, their shoulders stiff as they leaned toward each other, heads close together. It was almost like they were attempting to talk while staying as far away from each other as possible. The tension in her brother's body was noticeable even at a distance. Esmeralda sipped from her champagne as she watched them, intrigued by the discomfort in their body language. Such a striking difference from the warmth and ease she had with her own mother.

They were clearly in a heated conversation but there was no warmth there. Abruptly, Onyx backed away from his mother, his lighter complexion mottled with red. He looked angry as he stormed off, leaving Carmelina to glare at him. Whatever had passed between those two had not been a pleasant mother and son moment. Esme's eyes stayed on Carmelina's angry face for a second, but the woman stormed off in the direction of the stairs.

Esme's gaze returned to roaming the lavish garden until she found her other sibling. Unlike Esmeralda, who had gotten her coloring from their father, Perla Sambrano was fair and very slender, almost frail looking. She was beautiful, with cascading blond hair and piercing gray eyes. Tonight, she was dressed impeccably in a royal purple empire-waist gown, though she looked very small standing in a corner trying to capture the attention of a man who barely seemed to notice she was there. He was tall and commanding, dwarfing her with his height. She looked like she was pleading to him, but he barely looked at her, and after a few more attempts she gave up and walked away, swiping her fingers under her eyes.

As Perla briskly made her way to the exit she seemed to notice Esme, and for a moment she paused, hesitant. Esme's heart kicked around in her chest, curiosity and the need to feel seen by these people betraying her feigned indifference. Perla looked in her direction so intensely that for a second Esme thought she was going to walk over, to say something. But she didn't; her younger sister just lowered her gaze and left through one of the limestone arches. Esme didn't know what to make of the disappointment she felt when her sister walked away. Nothing was simple in this place, with this family. Every feeling only served to burst open another more complicated and unwanted one.

Esme stood there considering the tableau she'd just witnessed—and trying to untangle her feelings about all of it—when her phone buzzed in her clutch. She smiled sadly at the flurry of messages she had from her mother and her tías. She'd sent a selfie of herself in her green gown and their responses ranged from firework emojis to *bellísima*, *hermosa* and every other word for "beautiful" in Spanish they could come up with. It was a good reminder she had people who loved her waiting not far from here. People who had her back and would never leave her to cry alone in a corner, or speak angry words to her where everyone could see. She had something to prove to the Sambranos, but she didn't need their approval.

"Well, well, well…if it isn't my father's dirty little secret. Are you getting tired of pretending you belong here?" a very loud voice called in her direction. It took Esme a moment to react, but then she saw him. Onyx was sauntering up to her unsteadily as every eye in their vicinity turned toward her. Her face felt hot with embarrassment and she wanted to hide. She hated being a spectacle. But if Onyx thought he was going to hurl insults at her and she'd just take it, he had another thing coming.

"Nice to see you, Onyx. Did you have to take some time out from your busy schedule of photobombing celebrities to make it tonight?" She sounded like a bitch, but she didn't care.

"I hope you enjoy the free booze, because you won't be around much longer." From the slur in his words, it seemed he was enjoying the open bar enough for the both of them. "You will never be CEO of Sambrano. My mother will see to that." Her brother's mouth twisted into an ugly sneer as he looked at her with naked loathing. He really hated her, which shouldn't have been the surprise it was. On the couple of occasions her mother had sent her to spend time at their father's house, Onyx had barely acknowledged her.

He was just a couple of years younger than her and they'd both been small then—barely in elementary school—but she always remembered how he'd looked at her. Like she was something distasteful and unpleasant. Something he didn't like in his space. And it seemed like that feeling had only grown in the years since. That realization was a sucker punch. She'd expected defiance, even some territorial pettiness, but this hatred cut her. To know that people who shared her blood despised her without knowing much about her…

It hurt, but she would be damned if she let anyone see it.

"Sorry to inform you, brother, but Sambrano Studios is mine, too. That was how our father wanted it. Now you and I even own equal shares." She tipped her glass to him as if to toast the happy news, even as her stomach felt like it was trying to crawl up her throat. "Means you better get used to seeing me around." She avoided looking around, not wanting to see all the disapproving faces. She could agonize about it all later, but right now she would not give any of them the satisfaction.

Onyx looked even more furious. "You don't belong here. You're not his real daughter!" he spat, stalking closer. But before he could take another step toward her, Rodrigo yanked Onyx's arms so hard he lifted him off his feet.

"Don't even think about it!" Rodrigo whispered furiously, as he plucked her brother off his feet like a rag doll and proceeded to physically remove him from the room. She started after them as Onyx struggled in Rodrigo's grip, but it was pointless. Onyx was not a large man and he was certainly no match for six feet and two inches of solid muscle.

"Let me go." Her brother raged as Rodrigo made his way through the room, headed for the archway that led to an exit. You could hear a pin drop in the room, other than Onyx's enraged protests and the clicking of her stilettos as she followed the two men. Every single person in the room was frozen in fascination watching the drama unfold. She should've known this would happen. In the back of her mind it occurred to her that this was very much out of character for Rodrigo. The man hated messiness but here he was diving right into the fray. It was better not to dig too deeply into the why of his actions. She already had enough to deal with.

She wouldn't be surprised if a video of this shitshow wasn't on every New York City gossip website within the hour. From the corner of her eye she thought she saw Perla looking on as Rodrigo manhandled her brother. For a second she wondered if Carmelina would join this circus, and really give all these people the show of a lifetime. But Rodrigo moved fast and soon he was shoving Onyx through a door leading into a small alcove and propping the smaller man against the nearest wall.

"Rodrigo, put him down," she pleaded from a safe

distance, aware that getting between the two men was not advisable.

But it was like talking to a wall. He completely ignored her and continued to get in Onyx's face. If people could only see the cool, calm and collected Mr. Almanzar now. "Are you out of your damn mind, Onyx?"

"Get your hands off me," Onyx screeched, batting furiously at the tight grip Rodrigo had on his arm to no avail. When he wasn't able to make the taller man budge, Onyx looked around as if he could find someone to help him. When his eyes landed on Esme that familiar vicious expression returned to his face.

"Oh, I see how it is. You two are scheming together." He threw his head back and laughed. "Oh, honey, have you hitched your star to the wrong wagon. This one is a cold-blooded bastard. He only looks out for himself. If he's who you're counting on then we definitely have nothing to worry about." He twisted his mouth into what she assumed was a satisfied smile.

"I guess you do have something against people who work for a living, *little brother*." Esme knew the smartest move was to keep her mouth shut and let Rodrigo handle Onyx. But it incensed her to hear her brother talk about her ex-lover like that when he'd done so much to keep their father's company going. Rodrigo shot her a surprised look, then turned his attention back to Onyx when he tried to lunge for her.

"You don't know anything about me. About any

of us. You're not a part of this family." Onyx's ugly sneer disappeared when Rodrigo shook him hard, pressing him harder to the wall.

"Don't talk to her. You little shit, you're not good enough to lick her fucking boots." Onyx paled and even Esmeralda could hear the cold menace in Rodrigo's voice.

This was a freaking mess. Rodrigo was seconds from completely losing his temper and when he did this was truly going to go to hell in a handbasket. Onyx would make sure everyone knew what had happened and somehow she'd be blamed for it. She moved fast and got as close as she could without running the risk of getting elbowed in the face.

"Rodrigo, please stop," she asked with as much calm as she could manage. "He's not worth it. He's got nothing to lose. We do." She could see how the words landed by the way he ground his jaw. After a moment, he stepped back and released his grip on Onyx, who stumbled for a moment, but quickly began to run his mouth again.

"If you're sleeping with him, my advice is that you cut your losses now. He'll sell you out in a minute to stay on top."

"Are you trying to get your ass beat, Onyx?" Rodrigo growled. "I'm so fucking tired of you people and your drama." Onyx just weaved in place, that drunk smile on his face. They'd keep doing this all night until they came to blows or Onyx barfed, and she'd had enough.

You people. The loathing in Rodrigo's voice was like a slap in the face. He meant the Sambranos. He meant her, too.

"I didn't ask you to get involved in this, Rodrigo. I can take care of myself." She didn't even give him a chance to respond and moved toward the door. She was done with this. She needed to get back to what she was here to do: prove to the board she was the only one who could take the helm of the television empire.

Nine

"Why did you leave like that, Esmeralda?" Rodrigo sounded rough as he walked into Esmeralda's office, even to his own ears. He'd lost it back at the party, acted like a complete Neanderthal, and he couldn't even find it in himself to regret any of it. Well, that wasn't true. He regretted embarrassing Esmeralda. He was sorry he'd made an already bad situation worse for her, but when he'd seen that little shit coming for her, he'd gone into a rage.

"What was I supposed to stay there for, Rodrigo?" She sounded fed up, and he couldn't blame her. "As you can see, I'm working. What are you doing here? I thought you would've had enough Sambrano drama for the night." He had. He was absolutely *done* with

Onyx, Carmelina and their bullshit. But instead of going home like a sensible person, he'd ended up here. He'd told himself a dozen times on the drive over that he was here to finish up some work. But he'd been lying; he'd come after her, hoping she'd be here. To make sure she was all right. She'd been magnificent. Standing up for herself when anyone else would've cowered.

"I *am* tired of Sambrano drama." He should be thanking her for the way she'd stood up for him. No one had ever done that. Usually people were only too happy to see him be dressed down. They lived to remind him he was only the help. How easily they forgot that if it weren't for him things would've fallen apart. But they still despised him. Loathed him for being the only person Patricio trusted, as if that hadn't cost him anything. "I thought after that scene you'd want to call it a night."

She scoffed at that. "And then what? Let my so-called brother's insults scare me off? Carmelina Sambrano made sure I knew what my place was my entire life, and yet I am still here," she said, leaning against the desk chair. Her tone was placid, but there was a sharpness to the way she held herself that told him that scene at The Cloisters had shaken her. "I would never give any of them the satisfaction of thinking they got to me. Sorry, Rodrigo, you're going to have to work a little harder for that corner office."

"I already have a corner office." He sounded pissed and tired, but she wasn't fazed by any of it.

Her long neck and back were ramrod straight as she typed on the keyboard, her eyes darting between the three monitors in front of her. That's when he noticed she hadn't even bothered to change her clothes. She'd wiped off her makeup, put her hair up in a top bun, taken off her shoes and gotten to work.

Focused. Determined. She stayed on her path, didn't let the drama distract her. He'd lost that somewhere along the way. The ability to let all the scheming roll off his back. To the world he looked like he was made of stone, but he felt worn down. Sometimes he could barely come up with one or two reminders of why he loved this job. Being at the helm of a television empire came with power and prestige, but when everyone thought of you as the lackey, that you got the job by kissing ass, you had to constantly prove yourself. And he was tired of having to deal with the scorn of people who could not survive one day doing what he did. And in that at least he and Esmeralda had something in common.

Patricio ignored his daughter for her entire life. And yet of all his children she was the one who'd gotten his determination and ambition. The one who had pursued a career in television. And still she was the one who had to prove herself, who had to earn the right to claim her place. "What are you working on?" he asked, taking off his jacket as he came over to look at the screen. He needed a distraction.

She glanced up at him for a moment and he did not miss that her eyes landed right at the spot where he'd unbuttoned his shirt and a sliver of skin was peeking out. His eyes locked on her lips out of their own volition and his mouth watered with the memory of how it had felt to kiss her tonight. Despite the exhaustion, a jolt of desire coursed through his body at the thought of doing it again. He'd take that smart mouth with hard, hungry kisses and then he'd pick her up, wrap her strong legs around his waist and have her right against the wall. Lose himself in the tight perfect grip of her body, until they were both spent.

Get your head in the game, Rodrigo. She's about her business and you need to be, as well. He pulled up a chair and sat next to her as he rolled up his sleeves. Esmeralda gave him a suspicious look as he pointed at the slide she was working on. "Tell me about this."

"Are you serious?" she asked incredulously.

"The board already knows I can do the job. They want to see if you can."

She rolled her eyes at him, but something about what she saw on his face seemed to smooth the lines of tension on her forehead, and she turned to what he was asking her about.

"This is my Big Ask," she informed him, as her eyes scanned the screen. "I'm proposing we bring back some of the programming that Sambrano was known for in the early years. Remember the old comedy sketch shows they did with comedians from all over Latin America? The Afro-Latinx culture focused shows. I was also thinking that we could have a network dedicated to only Latinx food. And not just tacos and ceviche, which are the only things people seem to think we eat." Her eyes lit up as she talked, her hands everywhere as she explained, and he could not get enough of it, of her.

"I'm envisioning baking competitions, grilling showdowns. I'm talking Garifuna pastry chefs, Quechua bakers, Argentinian grill masters. I want every region, every country, *every culture* represented." With every word she said his brain woke up more, and he realized he was intrigued. He was more than intrigued. He was…energized. "There are so many Latinx chefs who have gained a huge following on Instagram and I bet would love to be on a network, you know?"

He frowned as she went through the slides, taking in some of her concepts. They were good. Innovative but still staying in line with the brand. The kind of stuff he'd pushed for in his early years at Sambrano but gave up on after getting shot down again and again.

Well, they weren't exactly like his. Her ideas were a lot bolder. Where his had been baby steps toward going back to the roots of Sambrano, she was proposing leaps. He'd suggested a cooking show; she was going in with a whole network. Then he looked down at the open folder on the desk and froze. "What's that?"

She looked down at where his finger was pointing

and then up at him, beaming, all the anger and resentment from earlier in the evening forgotten. That was something he'd always loved about her. Esmeralda could never stay angry for long.

"There's no cover letter, so I don't know who drafted the memo. It's almost eleven years old, but the concept is basically a prototype of what I'd like to propose." His heart sped up again as she continued. "Listen to this," she told him as she pointed to the paper. "'We have to continue to fulfill the promise we made to our viewers, that from Patagonia to Baja California, they can go home when they tune into Sambrano networks.'" The smile on her face was radiant as she looked up at him.

"That's it. That's the mission. We have to lean into the vision that our world is wide and rich enough that we could have entire cable networks fully dedicated to us. Like a Latinx History Channel. All our histories, bringing in Indigenous producers, Afro-descendant filmmakers. Shows dedicated to LGBTQ+ Latinx communities. We can do anything, like *Project Runway*, but make it Latinx." She grinned at him and he found himself smiling back. Seeing her vision clearly. "I want every gaze represented. To make a mark in the current landscape Sambrano has to think bigger. One channel isn't enough to carry all that we are." She was practically vibrating with excitement, her eyes on a future without limits. An artist standing in front of an empty canvas with a brush, paint and endless possibilities. And she was a force to be reckoned with.

"You were around then." She said it almost as if she'd just remembered that fact. "Do you have any idea who wrote this and if they're still here? I'd love to talk to them to find out why their ideas were never implemented."

He paused, nervous to confess this secret to her. "I wrote it." He almost laughed when she did a double take, as if she couldn't even picture it. He couldn't blame her. He could barely remember the twenty-five-year-old junior content developer who wrote that memo. When was the last time he'd felt that inspired? When he'd felt unafraid to launch himself into something just because he felt passionate about it? He couldn't recall.

"You?" she asked, her eyes wide with surprise.

He crossed his arms over his chest, feeling defensive and a little hurt at her astonishment. "Is it so hard to believe that I could've written that?"

Her eyes softened at whatever she saw in his face and tapped him on the shoulder. "Don't be such a baby. I'm just surprised, that's all. You've always seemed so…risk-averse."

"You mean boring," he said. She pointed a finger at him, clicking her tongue. "I'm a realist," he declared, doing his best to hide the peevishness in his tone.

She gave him a long look from under those thick dark lashes of hers and he could see the hint of a smile pulling up at her lips. "I meant solid, reliable. One who sticks to what works." She wasn't wrong. He'd learned to temper his ideas, to work within the confines of what was doable, and she would have to learn to, as well. He uncrossed his arms, feeling like he needed something to do with his hands, with his eyes. To keep from uttering something he shouldn't or worse, reaching out and touching her. Boundaries were his friend.

"I liked that about you," she said, almost ruefully. "Your steadiness." His chest expanded at her words, the sincerity in them. Esmeralda never said something she didn't mean. And that was what had always devastated him when it came to her. She would never lie, not even to protect her pride. He kept his mouth closed as he sensed his own onslaught of confessions coming on. No good could come of that.

They stayed with their gazes locked, and that need which seemed ever-present when he was around Esmeralda swirled like a ring of fire in his gut. Ten years of telling himself he was over her. That the entire relationship had been a mistake. That Esme had only been interested in him as a way to get back at her father. That there was nothing there. That he'd destroyed any chance of getting her back. That they were both *better off.* Each of those lies turned to dust the moment he'd seen her again and were immediately replaced by this feckless want.

"What ever happened to the guy who wrote

this?" she asked, and there was a breathlessness to her voice.

"That guy learned idealism got him nowhere. That to get to the top he had to compromise." And now that he was at the top, he wondered if those compromises might have been too high of a price to pay.

"I think you're lying."

"You know me a lot less than you think you do, Esmeralda," he rebuffed, voice tight with too much feeling.

"I know that the same guy who wrote this memo was the guy I was falling in love with. I know that even though you let my father and his shitty dog-eat-dog view of the world suck you in, you're the guy who helped your family when they lost everything. You might have turned your back on that man, but he's still there." Her finger pressed right on the spot in his chest where his heart was pounding like a jackhammer.

He stood up, shaking from the way her words had struck him. "I'm heading out for the night."

"You know what else I know?" she asked, voice dripping with something that made him stop in his tracks. "That you're dying to finish what we started in that creepy bedroom suite this afternoon." He had to suppress a laugh even as his cock hardened from her words.

"And the last thing I know is that I'd let you… All you have to do is ask."

His hazel-eyed beauty bit her bottom lip, tucked

a curl behind her ear as she waited for his reaction. It had been stupid to kiss her. Stupid and potentially disastrous because the floodgates were now wide open. He'd known he would do it again if she asked him. He'd been dizzy with the possibility of it. And now she had.

Hope had always come at a steep cost for Rodrigo, and he had never paid a higher price than when he'd let himself believe he could have Esmeralda Sambrano-Peña. He'd sworn he'd never again take a gamble like the one he'd taken on this woman. And yet here he was, ten years later, older but clearly not much wiser, about to plunge into the abyss again.

Ten

"If we start this, we're not stopping until I've had you, Esmeralda," he warned, already moving toward her. In an instant he'd gone from feeling a bone-deep weariness to a madness that crackled under his skin like lightning. Some things never changed, and Esmeralda had a knack for making him forget he was supposed to be measured and stoic.

"Did I stutter, Rodrigo?" He didn't say a word, he just leaned in and scooped her into his arms, and after a yelp of surprise she wrapped her legs around his waist and held on. "Why can't I keep my hands off you?" she grumbled as she worked on kissing down his neck, her hands already busy with the buttons of his shirt.

He grunted when she used her teeth on him and wished he could sprint to his office without risking ramming into a glass door. The lights of the entire floor were off except for the small lamp on Esme's desk and the ceiling light guiding him to the bedroom in his office. Patricio was probably rolling over in his grave right now, but even that thought would not stop him from doing this.

He was tired of holding back, of not letting himself have the things he wanted. The things he craved. Only with Esmeralda had he ever let go, cut loose every one of his passions, and she'd always met him each step of the way. She quenched his every thirst, and it had been so long since he'd felt this kind of urgency. He'd been walking in a desert these past ten years without her. He'd known what was missing, but his need to never step out of line, to stay on track, kept him from her. It had been unfair of Patricio to ask him to stay away from her, but none of that mattered here and now.

He reached the door to the suite in a few swift steps and slammed his hand on the button that would slide it open. Esme tried to loosen the grip of her legs around his waist and pushed off him like she was intending to walk the rest of the way. He was not having it. A sound very much like a growl escaped from his chest as he crushed her to him. "You're staying right here." He pressed the point by lowering his head and licking into her mouth.

"Why do I find this side of you so ridiculously

hot?" she asked, feigning annoyance at the same time she slid a hand down to his crotch and gripped his hard cock over his pants. "Mmm, looks like someone is ready to unleash himself on me." She bit his earlobe as he reached a serviceable surface and set her down. She kept her legs around him, but now that his hands were free, he let them explore.

"Mess around and find out, Esmeralda," he warned, eliciting a wicked laugh from her.

"I'm planning to, Rodrigo." She was a brat and he loved it. He had to breathe through the need pounding inside him. He pulled back for a second. There was one small light in the bathroom, so that she was cast in shadow. But he could see her leonine eyes, like embers in the dark. Full of the heat that had always burned him down to ashes.

"I want to be right here." His voice was gravel as he cupped her heat. She writhed against him, gasping from his touch, but he wanted to see her undone. "I'm going to be so deep inside you," he told her as he nipped her earlobe, coaxing a delicious little moan from her. "But first I'm going to make you scream for me." He brought one hand to her breast, and tweaked a taut nipple, just like he remembered drove her wild. Her chest was heaving, and he could feel her need in the way she moved against him. "Once I've made you come on my tongue."

"Rodrigo." She sounded needy and the urge to give her whatever she asked for was almost overpowering. But he wanted to take this slow, savor it and do all the things he'd yearned for and could not have for so long. With agonizing gentleness he took her face in his hands, brought their faces closer, so their lips brushed against each other. He flicked out his tongue for a taste.

"Don't tease me, dammit," she protested, making him smile.

"So impatient, Joya," he teased, before going in for a rough kiss. He ate at her mouth. Their tongues tangled together in a frantic dance. He felt greedy and he already knew he would never get enough of Esmeralda. He'd been starving, taking scraps when this was the only thing that could fill him. He felt the oxygen like fizz in his lungs, every cell replenished from finally getting what he'd needed.

Her. Only her.

His hands drifted down to undo the zipper at her back, then made quick work of her bra while he grazed her throat with his teeth. "Tell me what you want," he demanded, cupping her naked breasts, his cock getting impossibly harder just from feeling the heft of them. He couldn't resist grazing the flat of his tongue against one nipple and then the other one. He could devour her and still it would not be enough.

"You," she whispered before taking his hand and placing it against her hot sex.

"Is this where you want me?" he asked while sliding his hand under her skirts, looking for her wet heat. He felt the silkiness of her skin as his palms moved over her thighs. He sucked in a breath when he reached her core and discovered what was waiting for him. “Where are your panties, Esmeralda?” He could not sound mad if he tried.

She pressed a smile to his neck and nodded. “I showered before the reception and didn’t exactly have a change of clothes here.” Her tone was casual, but he could hear that she was very pleased with herself for undoing him. Roughly, he picked her up again until her feet hit the floor and helped her step out of her dress. He was about to toss it to the side, but she stopped him before he balled up the fabric.

“Oh no you don’t. That’s Siriano. Place it on the armchair, *gently*.” It was extremely hard to focus with her completely naked in front of him. But he did as she asked, then took her by the hand and led her to the bed.

“So beautiful,” he said, once she was on her back, laid out for him like an offering. He used his hands to spread her legs and admired her for a moment. He’d missed this. Ten years of making do when he knew this bounty was out there. All that flawless brown skin, for him to touch, to lick, to suck, to claim. With two fingers he parted her folds and placed his lips right at her core, tongue darting out to taste her.

“Don’t stop.” He’d always loved how demanding she was. That her self-consciousness flew out the window whenever he had his mouth and hands on her. That he could make her lose herself in pleasure. She groaned and fisted his hair in her hands—moving against him as he worked to pleasure her, and the little moans and gasps she made set his blood on fire. The taste of her was intoxicating, filling all his senses until she was all he could hear, taste, see and smell. Soon she was bucking against his mouth, cries of ecstasy piercing the silence of the room.

"I've missed your mouth," she whispered breathlessly, as she ran her hands over his shoulders and back, pointy nails softly grazing his sensitized skin. He shivered from the onslaught of emotions.

"I missed everything," he confessed, losing himself to her touch, mouth pressing kisses to her warm skin as he made his way up her body. He'd had relationships since her. He'd had lovers. So why did it feel like he'd gone a decade without human touch? Why did it feel like these were the first hands he'd had on him in years? His skin was parched, dry earth, and her hands were rain.

"I need you. Please, Rodrigo." Her words seemed so loud in the quiet room. He felt a tightening at his waist as she unbuttoned his trousers and unzipped them, and when he opened his eyes she was looking up at him, unrestrained hunger flashing in her eyes. Within seconds he was on her, his larger body covering hers. Skin on skin, fused together. There was nothing that could stop him from what they were about to do.

He reached for the side table where he'd left his shaving kit and plucked out a condom and rolled it on as she undulated on the bed, pleasuring herself. Her lusty moans resounded through the room and if he didn't get inside her he would combust. As soon as he was ready, he went in for another kiss, their tongues sliding together.

"More," she demanded as he placed himself right at her entrance. "Now, Rodrigo." He could not deny her or himself any longer and entered her.

"God," he gasped, heart pounding in his chest as pleasure coiled around his spine like a vise. "You're perfect. I want to be inside you forever." With one hand he moved them until her hips were canted just right and he could be seated to the hilt.

"Ah. I love this!" she cried as he pounded into her and she met him stroke for stroke. He placed a hand in between them and rubbed circles over her clit, desperate to feel her walls tighten around him. "I'm coming," she gasped, pulsing around him. And soon his orgasm was crashing over him as they shared hard, hungry kisses.

Yes, this was what he'd been missing. And as ill-advised and possibly disastrous as this was, with this woman warm and sated in his arms, he could not find it in him to regret it.

Eleven

"Hey, Mami," Esme answered the phone, her jaw cracking from a yawn.

"Mija, I never heard you get home last night, and this morning you left before I woke up!"

"I got in really late. I didn't want to wake you." Heat flooded her face as she thought of the reason why she'd gotten home at almost 2:00 a.m. "I ended up coming back to the office after the reception to um…" She cleared her throat as an image of Rodrigo with his head between her legs flashed through her mind. She closed her eyes, hoping to shut it down, but more moments from the night before came to her in a flurry of very not-safe-for-work images.

It had been supremely unwise to sleep with Rodrigo, but she could still feel the delicious aches from last night in her muscles. Yeah, that had been dumb, and so damn good. He was so strong. The way he'd taken her…his massive chest covering her as he surged into her. Over the years she'd convinced herself that being with Rodrigo had not been as earth-shattering as she'd remembered. That she'd embellished their time together because he'd been her first and she'd been in love with him for so long she created a fantasy in her head. She'd convinced herself that no one could be that good. Well, she'd been lying to herself, because the memory didn't hold a candle to the real thing.

The twenty-six-year-old gentle and attentive lover she'd been with at twenty-one was still there, but this Rodrigo was more skilled. Self-possessed like he was in every other aspect of his life. Although the restraint he carried himself with had evaporated the moment he put his hands on her. And his body, mercy. The man's chest was like sculpted, bronzed marble. Her very own flesh-and-bone lustful god who'd made her tremble in his hands.

"Esmeralda Luisa Sambrano Peña." Her mother's recitation of her full name made her jump in her seat. Her face heated again as she realized she'd been having sex daydreams while she had her mother on the phone.

"Sorry, Mami." *What was she doing?* "I just have a lot to do. I need like eight weeks and have four days, so I'm feeling the pressure to be here as much as possible."

"I hear you, but Esme, amor, don't start doubting yourself. You've been working hard for years for an opportunity like this. And you know what to do. Did that woman bother you again?"

"No. I haven't seen Carmelina." She sighed, feeling unsteady. She'd texted her mom about her father's widow showing up in Rodrigo's office. Esme wasn't planning on letting her know about the scene Onyx had made at the reception. That would only worry her. But Ivelisse's question was also a good reminder that she was on her own here. No matter how nice it had been to feel like Rodrigo was on her side, she *was* still trying to take his job. They were *not* on the same team.

She needed to get her head in the game or she would blow her chance to finally make her professional dreams come true. She had a moment with Rodrigo, and the mind-blowing sex was a way to blow off steam. A onetime thing that could not happen again and that was that. Closure. That's what it was, one last goodbye. And she hoped if she kept repeating that to herself she would eventually believe it.

"Good. If she bothers you again tell Rodrigo. He's a good boy and he'll help you." Esme rolled her eyes, because despite everything her mom still had a soft spot for him. She'd been the only one who'd known about their relationship back then, and even when Esmeralda called her mother to tell her how Rodrigo ended things, her mother had not disparaged him. She'd comforted Esmeralda and sat through many pity parties over the phone. But her mother had not spoken ill of him, not once.

"I'm trying to take his job, Mami. He's not exactly an ally. And let's not talk about how he ghosted me ten years ago."

Her mother clicked her tongue, a definite sign she did not approve of Esme's opinion of the man. "You should give him more credit. He's not a bad man. He's just loyal to a fault."

At least on that they agreed. "Yeah, and his loyalties are not with me. So, I need to keep my guard up. That means Rodrigo Almanzar is the enemy until I have the CEO position secured."

"Good morning to you, too, Ms. Sambrano-Peña."

Shit.

"Oh, hey." Yeah, there was no masking the "just got caught disparaging your name" guilt in her voice. From the look on his face he must've heard her fighting words. Dammit. Her and her big mouth. This was not the way to keep things civil. Sure, she didn't want to keep going down the path they started on last night, but she didn't want him mad at her, either. First she'd slept with him and now he'd found her talking smack about him behind his back. This was not a good development. She pointed at her earbuds. "It's Mami. Let me just end the call."

His face was back to that stony expression she could not read at all, the heat she'd seen in his eyes the night before replaced by a flinty stare. "I'm not here to chitchat, just wanted to remind you we're meeting with the CFO in ten minutes."

A hole opened in her chest at the detached way he spoke to her. Like she was nothing to him. As if last night had never happened. But wasn't this exactly what she wanted? Some distance. She'd told herself a dozen times since they'd parted ways last night she couldn't get caught up in her old baggage about Rodrigo. That she had to keep pushing to get her presentation ready. And it seemed they were on the same page. So this was great. Exactly what needed to happen. Then why did she feel like a ball of lead had settled in the pit of her stomach?

Because Rodrigo always did this to her. He made her weak and careless then he left her alone and discarded. Was she really going to set herself up to have her heart stomped like the last time? How could she forget how it had felt when he'd dumped her? God, and she'd slept with him. Not even 48 hours of having the man back in her life, and she had already broken every rule she'd set for herself with Rodrigo Almanzar. And she wanted to be angry, she wanted to be *furious*. But the way he'd touched her last night, the way he'd whispered in her ear that he'd ached for her, what those words had done to her—*that* would not be so easy to forget.

"Your office?" she asked as her mind raced.

He frowned at whatever he saw in her face, and for a moment she thought he'd say something about last night. That he'd mention the dozens of kisses they'd shared before they said goodbye. But instead, he uttered a clipped "Yes," and walked out.

The meeting was brutal and not for the reasons Esme had anticipated. Magdalena Polanco, their CFO, was great, and gave Esmeralda the rundown on all operating costs for the studio like she'd requested. Numbers people always intimidated her. Esmeralda's forte was more the big picture, the overarching vision, and not so much the intricacies of how to make that all work. But Magdalena seemed easy to work with, and Esme thought it would be nice to have someone like that on her team. A strong Latina who had gotten to the top of her field by working hard. At any other time she would've loved to pick her brain for an hour, ask Magdalena about her career trajectory, but Rodrigo's whole vibe was driving Esme nuts.

He'd barely acknowledged her during the meeting. And whenever she directed a question at him, he either answered with a monosyllable or he politely deferred to Magdalena. It was irritating as hell.

Was he going to ice her out for the next four days because she was trying to keep things professional? What the hell was his problem? They were grown adults who'd gotten a bit carried away after a stressful day—*surely* they could be cordial. Granted, it would be so much easier if he didn't look so damn good. He'd shaved this morning, but she could still feel every spot where his scruff had scraped the sensitive skin of her thigh when he was…

"Miss Sambrano-Peña?"

Dammit, she'd done it again. "I'm sorry." She tried to smile, but it would not quite take, so she just gave up. "What were you saying?"

"Just wondering if you had any other questions for me?"

She shook her head and resisted placing her palms on her flaming cheeks. "Nope. Thank you so much. I have everything I need for now. If I have a question I can give you a call, right?"

Magdalena gave her a warm smile as she stuffed papers back into her binder. "Absolutely. You have all my contact information and Rodrigo knows how to find me if it's something urgent." The older woman smiled affectionately at the object of Esmeralda's fevered musings.

"Tell Guille I'll call him this week. We said we'd go shoot some hoops." Magdalena beamed at Rodrigo.

"My youngest son was a teammate of Rodrigo's in college." Magdalena informed Esmeralda. "He's the one who recommended me for this job, you know?" Esme wondered if Magdalena was letting her know that as a way to tell her whose side she was on. But the way she looked at Rodrigo told her that wasn't it at all. She just genuinely liked him.

As much as Esmeralda wanted to act like a jerk

right now, she only smiled. "He made a smart move then, I can tell you're great at your job."

"He's fought for a lot people in his time here," she told Esme, before walking out of the office.

"You certainly have a lot of admirers amongst the corporate team."

Rodrigo lifted his gaze from whatever he was doing on his phone and stared at her for so long she wondered if he'd heard her. Irrational possessiveness was truly not her friend. And yet here she was, acting like he was her man, never mind that Magdalena had to be pushing seventy.

"You're jealous of Magdalena now? She has grandkids your age."

"Jealous? Please, you're so conceited." Now she sounded like a brat. His mouth twitched, but before it could turn into a smile he bit his bottom lip, and God, she wanted to lean over and suck on it. To sit astride his lap and kiss him senseless.

"You *sound* jealous, Esmeralda. I thought I was the enemy." Okay, so he *had* heard her.

She lifted a shoulder, trying very hard to feign an indifference she was not at all feeling. "You kind of are. We're at odds right now and it would do us both good not to forget that."

He arched an eyebrow at her words, and he looked so composed and controlled in that moment. Every hair in its place. His bespoke suit a perfect fit. He looked every inch the CEO. He looked like the man who should be sitting in this office. And that insidious insecurity flooded her. She wanted to lead this company. To prove—to the board, to her father's widow, to her siblings—that her father's wishes hadn't been born out of misguided guilt, but because she was the right person to run the studio.

But she wondered if she really had what it took to take the job from Rodrigo.

As she digested this fresh dose of conflicting feelings his phone buzzed, and after looking at it he stood purposefully, then waved a hand toward the door. "Go to your office and grab what you need for the rest of the day. We're going somewhere."

"What do you mean?" she asked, irritated at his attempt to order her around.

As usual he didn't give her anything. He just walked over to his desk and picked up a leather messenger bag. "I want you to see something."

She was annoyed at how vague he was being and a little hurt he hadn't brought up the night before. But she wasn't going to be a hypocrite and get mad. She had no intention of mentioning it, either.

She tried her best to give him a sincere smile when she glanced up at him. "Aren't you going to at least give me a hint? You know I hate surprises."

He stepped up to her, close enough that she could feel the heat of his body. He bent down so that his lips were almost grazing her ears. "You're just going to have to trust me, Joya."

Damn the man for being so infuriatingly enticing, and for the husky laugh he let out as she stood there shivering. She should've told him to cut it out. To stop playing games with her. But when she looked closely, she saw that he was far from unbothered. His shoulders were tense, and his eyes wary. He was holding himself as if he expected her to say she could never trust him—but that would be a lie. She thought of his easy friendship with Jimena, and Magdalena's clear affection and respect for him as evidence of the way that he carried himself personally *and* professionally. Yeah, despite everything, she still trusted Rodrigo Almanzar. And there was a simple reason for that: her mother was right; he *was* a good man.

Twelve

"The Grand Palace? Is it even open at noon on a weekday?" Rodrigo had to bite the inside of his cheek at Esmeralda's question. She'd been peppering him with them the entire thirty-minute drive uptown. She'd never liked being kept in the dark and it probably made him a jerk that he was enjoying seeing her practically vibrate from curiosity.

The driver stopped in front of the main entrance of the theater where the curator for the Latinx Diaspora Film and Television Archives was waiting for them. He turned to her and bit back the smile threatening to appear on his face. She looked so damn edible with that scowl on her face. He was so tempted to lean in and kiss all that annoyance right out of her. "It's open for us. There's something I want you to see."

He pushed open the door to the town car, but she would not budge. "No, tell me what we're doing here first."

He crossed his arms, mirroring hers. "Terca."

"You're the stubborn one. Just tell me."

He shook his head smiling and reached for her hand. "Ven. There's someone waiting for us," he told her and pointed at the curator who was patiently waiting for them to get out of the car.

"Fine," she groused as Rodrigo stepped out of the car and helped her do the same. Once they both had their feet firmly planted on the pavement, he had to force himself to let go of her hand.

"Señor Almanzar." The curator walked over to them, a welcoming smile on his face. "And this must be Ms. Sambrano."

"Sambrano-Peña," she corrected the man in a friendly tone. Rodrigo admired that in Esmeralda—she knew who she was. And nothing would change that. Not even losing the CEO position.

Rodrigo extended his hand to the man and made introductions. "Esmeralda, this is Huchi Piera. He's the curator and archivist for the theater and he's been kind enough to prepare some footage that I think will be helpful for your presentation." He saw when his words landed and for a fleeting moment a genuinely pleased smile appeared on her face. The realization that Rodrigo had done something to help her.

And he wished he could tell her what he was really thinking. That he'd woken up wanting her. That he could not get last night out of his head even for a second. That he'd almost had to jerk off in his office, because he still had her smell on his hands. That he was desperate to know if she was thinking about it, too. He wished he could ask if what he'd overheard her tell her mother had been true, or if, like him, she was just trying and failing to keep her feelings in check. But instead, he gestured toward the entrance.

"Shall we?" His tone was a little sharper than he intended. But when she looked at him, her eyes were wide and her mouth parted just a little. She looked excited and touched by him bringing her here, and it was getting harder to not give in to his instincts. To not bring her close, or place a hand at her back, so Piera and anyone else in the theater could see she was his.

"This way, Ms. Sambrano-Peña," Piera called, breaking the spell between them. By the next second she was all business, turning to follow the curator to the private screening area he'd prepared for them.

"Have you been to a show here before?" the curator asked as they crossed the large foyer of the theater and took a set of winding stairs up to a mezzanine.

"Yes. I have, many times," she said as she looked around. The Grand Palace was a gorgeous old theater, built in 1930 by the renowned architect Thomas W. Lamb. The sumptuous filigree carvings on the walls were exquisitely done and made it one of the most beautiful theaters in Manhattan. "It's such a beautiful building. The last time I was here, I brought my mom to see Johnny Ventura," Esmeralda said, slowly taking it all in, pausing to admire the beauty of the place. She'd always been like that, an admirer of other people's craft. Reverent when she was in front of true artistry.

Piera made an approving sound at the mention of the legendary Afro-Dominican merenguero. "Those were excellent shows."

"I missed that one," Rodrigo explained. "I wanted to come, but..." He was going to say he was working, which he had been, but he didn't want to talk about the office. "I never got around to getting tickets."

"Next time let your novia handle the tickets. My wife is always a lot more organized about that sort of thing than I am."

The older man calling Esme his girlfriend flustered him so much he missed the last step and almost fell flat on his face at the landing. When he got his footing back, he shook his head in her direction. "She's not my girlfriend."

As soon as the words were out of his mouth, he knew he'd made a mistake. Esmeralda stiffened at his harsh tone. "Wow, you'd think he just accused you of something." With that she turned to Piera. "We're not dating. In fact, we're barely friends."

Piera raised an eyebrow and stopped just beyond the doors to the small screening room. "Of course. My mistake." He didn't sound sorry at all. He was at that age when Latinx people said whatever they wanted with impunity and lived for getting their noses in people's business. "But you really should consider it. You make a very elegant couple."

Rodrigo swallowed down the growl in his throat and pointed at the open double doors in front of them. "Is this it?"

The curator gave him that shameless old man grin and nodded. "Yes, everything is ready for you." He winked at Rodrigo as if they were in on the same joke, then he turned to Esmeralda. "I've left copies of some old photographs that we have from when your dad did *Navidad Para el Pueblo* here at the theater." A beatific smile appeared on the old man's face at the mention of the free concerts for the Latinx community in New York City that Patricio had sponsored for decades. "Your father was a great man, and a true champion of our culture. He saved the theater in the '90s when developers wanted to tear it down. Did you know that?"

Esme gasped at Piera's revelation and turned to Rodrigo, an eyebrow raised in question. Her voice trembled ever so slightly when she finally spoke. "I had no idea."

Rodrigo felt a stinging in the back of his throat as he took in Esme's reaction. He'd been so caught up in getting through this week that he'd forgotten this was not just a competition for Esmeralda, this was her chance to finally reclaim a part of her she'd been denied her whole life.

Piera smiled kindly at Esmeralda. “Mr. Sambrano quietly did many things for a lot of groups looking to conserve and document the culture of the diaspora. That’s what the footage you’ll see showcases. It’s a shame the documentary was never finished.”

“We’re watching the footage from the documentary? I thought that—” Esme asked, looking between Piera and himself.

“I’ll take it from here. Thank you, Mr. Piera.”

The old man dipped his head again and pointed at some doors that were visible from the balcony in the mezzanine. “My offices are down there. You can come get me once you’re done. We’ve left everything you asked for in the screening room. You’re all alone up here, so if you need anything you can call down from the phone that’s inside. Just dial zero. It was a pleasure meeting you, Ms. Sambrano-Peña.” With that he left them standing alone together.

“After you.” Rodrigo stood awkwardly in front of Esmeralda, gesturing toward the door. And it seemed he could not stop himself from sounding like an ass.

She narrowed her eyes at him, but her curiosity seemed to win out and she finally stepped inside.

“Is this the stuff that Carmelina swore I would not touch?” she asked mischievously.

“That’s exactly what it is.” He was grinning now, especially because Esme was giving him one of those “I don’t want to be impressed, but I still am” looks.

“I assumed she had called anyone who could let me see the footage to warn them off.”

"Carmelina thinks the only way to win is to be a bully," he said with a wave of his hand. "People do what she says not out of respect, but fear. The only way someone like me gets ahead is remembering that relationships are the biggest asset I have."

He lifted a shoulder, looking around the small room as she digested his words. "A few years ago, when the theater needed some funds to buy equipment to keep their archives in a climate-controlled space, I helped them. When Carmelina forbade the studio from giving you access to the footage, I remembered Piera had asked for copies to keep in the archives. So, I called in a favor."

"That's pretty devious, Rodrigo Almanzar," she said, a tiny conspiratorial smile forming on her lips.

"I'm not just a pretty face, Esmeralda," he joked, eliciting a laugh from her as he guided her to the front of the room. His hand pressed to the small of her back as she took everything in. The room was small, with only about a dozen large plush reclining chairs facing a large screen. There was a table at the front of the room laden with the things he'd ordered.

He knew the moment she saw it because she did a double take. "Is that…mofongo and champagne?" she asked as a goofy grin appeared on her face.

"It's lunchtime. And El Malecón is right across the street. It used to be your favorite," he said soberly, but it was getting harder and harder not to match her delighted expression.

She clicked her tongue as she took the few steps

to the table, inhaling as she reached it. It did smell amazing. "It's very hard to remember we're supposed to be archrivals when you're being this nice."

Rodrigo seriously gave her whiplash. One moment he looked horrified at the suggestion that they were a couple and the next he's walking her into a private theater with her favorite dish and champagne on a literal silver platter.

"Who pairs plantains and Moët, Rodrigo?" she asked, feigning an annoyance she didn't feel while he poured her some of the chilled bubbly.

"Bougie Dominicans, Esmeralda," he quipped as he passed her the glass, and she could see the smile tugging at the side of his own mouth.

She raised the glass to her lips and it occurred to her the fizz of the bubbles were already under her skin before the liquid touched her lips. Rodrigo always did that to her, made her body effervescent with energy. One look, one word and she could forget all the ways in which he was never a good idea. But one thing she could not deny was that he got her. Rodrigo understood what made her tick like no one else ever had. And this ridiculous and perfect lunch choice was only further evidence of that. Again the questions balled up in her throat.

Are we going to just walk away from each other again? Are we going to let my victory steal this from us? Are you not feeling like your world got turned upside down last night, too?

But she didn't ask a single one. She would not spill her guts just to have Rodrigo pick Sambrano Studios over her…again. "I guess it is lunchtime, we might as well eat," she said a little too brightly, reaching for one of the little white plates next to the platters of food. She placed a ball of mashed plantains and chicharron on it. Then she sat down on the stool he'd pulled out for her.

"I know what happens when you get hangry," he teased as she took a big bite.

"Jerk," she grumbled through a mouthful of mofongo, but she was too content for it to hold any real animosity. "Mmm…perfect mofongo is perfect."

He nodded, looking a bit too pleased with himself, as he watched her eat. She felt the heat from his stare warm her skin. But in the next moment he settled down with his lunch, and soon they were both tucking into the delicious food. Once she was done, she poured herself a fresh glass of bubbly and walked over to one of the plush leather armchairs in front of the gigantic screen.

Rodrigo fussed around for a moment, pushing the small table to a corner of the room. Then he turned off the lights, leaving them in total darkness for a moment before the screen lit up.

She turned around to look at him, but she could only make out his shadow as he walked over to her. "I'm nervous," she confessed, as conflicting emotions swirled through her. Rodrigo's eyes softened at her confession, and even if everything about these last few days felt murky and confusing, she knew he got why she was feeling that way.

"It'll be good, Joya," he said, reaching for her hand. And dammit, that was exactly what she needed. Something to ground her. And with his strong hand clutching hers she felt ready. He'd been this person for her so many times in her life. And she would be lying to herself if she didn't recognize that she'd missed his steadiness. The way he seemed to almost instinctually knew what to say or do.

"Are you ready?" he asked so gently it was barely a whisper.

She nodded as tears crawled up her throat, but the sound of her father's voice saved her from having to say anything other than a hoarse thank-you. She sat back to watch the oral history of what her father had built. It was a whirlwind of emotions, so much sadness and regret for what she never got to say to or ask him. She wished he could've been a different man, but right beside that disappointment there was admiration and an undeniable affinity.

The thirtysomething Patricio Sambrano who had set out to create something that had never been done before really was a kindred spirit. There was a fire in those brown eyes Esmeralda recognized at a bone-deep level. She may not have been the child he raised or recognized, but his ambition and drive were in her blood. He'd dreamed big and made it happen and she would do the same.

By the time the screen went dark she was dizzy

with the onslaught of ideas the interviews and footage had given her. Rodrigo had been right, this was exactly what she needed to see to finally get the pieces of what she would present the board to come together. She'd known what she wanted for the future of Sambrano, and in a way it eased her to know that the Patricio from the early days would likely approve of her choices. Even though he'd let her down, he'd left her a legacy that was worth preserving. More than that, she wanted to finish what Patricio had set out to do and had not managed to achieve: make Sambrano Studios a representation of all that Latinx people were.

She turned to Rodrigo, who was still quietly sitting beside her, and all she felt was a wave of overwhelming gratitude. No one else would've done this for her. But he'd known, he understood why she needed to see these interviews. Even after a two-minute conversation last night he'd known. He'd done what was best for her, even when it meant hurting his own chances to stay on as CEO.

Rodrigo Almanzar really was a good man. Before she could talk herself out of it, she leaned over and kissed him. "Thank you," she whispered against his lips. She had too many emotions coursing through her to find the right words. Without wasting any time he brought her to his lap, deepening the kiss. And soon the soft grateful embrace turned into something torrid and urgent.

His chest rumbled with a possessive sound and

his fingers gripped her waist. “Rodrigo.” She gasped, already so caught up in him she could barely remember where she was. She ground herself against him, feeling his hardness against her core, just a few layers of fabric keeping her from what she needed. She was astride him now, knees on either side of his muscular thighs, rocking into him, needy and urgent.

“Unbutton your blouse,” he ordered, and that commanding growl made wet heat pool at the apex of her thighs. “I want to see your breasts.”

“Someone could come in,” she said, hands already undoing the first button.

“No one’s coming here unless I call for them. Unlike you, other people usually obey my requests,” he told her with a smirk, his eyes zeroed in on her chest as he slid a hand under her flowy skirt and ran a rough palm from her knee up to the juncture of her thighs, his fingers skimming along the edge of her panties. “Do you want me here?” he asked, two fingers stroking at the seam of her pussy over the lacy material of her underwear.

“I do,” she whispered.

“I can feel how hot and wet you are.” His voice was dripping with sex and that edge of raw possessiveness that drove her wild. Rodrigo touched her like he owned her, and that’s how he kept her coming back.

“Touch me.” She gasped as the roughness of the lace grazed her clit, her hips grinding into his hand of their own volition. Without taking his gaze off her, he roughly pulled down her underwear. Two digits deftly parted her folds and soon he was circling that nub of nerves until her skin was on fire. "Pull down your bra. I want to suck on your nipples."

"Ahh..." She couldn't form words. Her body was aflame with need and pleasure. It should annoy her how he could work her into a frenzy with just a few deft touches. Instead, she slid the straps off her shoulders and pushed down her bra, just like he'd asked. She felt so exposed, but she wanted what he was giving her, *needed it.* This felt illicit and thrilling and heaven help her, she would not stop.

"Put your hands on my shoulders, lean in. Oh yeah," he said, low and dirty. "You need this bad."

She did, she really did. He turned his face up as he worked her with his hands. He licked up the valley between her breasts, tongue flat and rough on her skin, making her shiver.

"You were always so sensitive here," he muttered, lips grazing her nipples. His tongue darted out, flicking the pebbled peaks, just like his fingers were flicking her core. He sucked on her and caressed her until her whole world reduced to the pleasure he was giving her. "Come for me, Joya," he demanded, and she did, tremors racking her body as her orgasm crashed over her.

She wrapped her arms around his neck and pressed her face to the crook of it. Esmeralda had been kidding herself earlier, telling herself this was closure, that she was over it. The only way that lie could survive was if she never saw him again. As long as Rodrigo reached for her, she would keep succumbing.

"We're a mess," she muttered, lips pressed to his skin. He circled his strong arms around her and laughed ruefully.

"I'm sure Piera would ban us for life for desecrating the sanctity of the private screening room." She could hear the smile in his voice.

"We are extremely indecent," she agreed. "These interludes are going to make it hard to enjoy taking your job." The moment the words came out of her mouth Rodrigo stiffened under her and released her from his embrace.

"Yeah. We got a bit carried away there. We really have to stop doing that," he said harshly as she worked on getting her bra back to rights and her blouse buttoned. "I'm glad you're aware none of this changes anything. I'll help you find the information you need, Esmeralda, but I have no intention of stepping down as CEO."

It was like a bucket of cold water, but she'd needed it. This was who they were now. At odds, being pulled apart even when they could not stay away from each other. In that moment she resented her father for putting her in this position, and she wished—she really wished—that for once Rodrigo could pick her. But he wouldn't; Sambrano Studios was the love of his life, the only thing that he'd sacrificed everything for again and again. He'd never give it up.

She smoothed her skirts and felt her face heat with embarrassment as she felt a wet spot right where he'd cupped her sex. She'd been so aroused she'd soaked the fabric. She was embarrassing herself. *He* was not letting his lust interfere with his plans and she had to do she same. She grabbed her purse before stepping into the aisle then turned to look at him. She hated that even after just having him, she still wanted him. That even when she despised him, she craved how he made her feel.

"My plan is to be CEO, Rodrigo. You giving me a few orgasms is not going to change that."

Thirteen

Esmeralda had stomped out of the theater after thanking Piera and got into the car without saying a word. "Could you please have the driver drop me off at my apartment? I have what I need and can work the rest of the day from home. I don't want to go back to Sambrano."

Usually someone not wanting to talk suited him just fine, but as usual, his reaction to anything and everything that had to do with Esmeralda was far from his normal. "So you're not going to acknowledge me?" He tried to keep his tone mild, but every one of his emotions was set at the maximum. He felt out of control, frustration building in him like an avalanche. He was out of sorts, regretful for ruining the moment, for reacting like he had at her words. He should just leave this alone, drop her off at home and get on with his day.

"Manny, we're taking Ms. Esmeralda home. 419 Riverside Drive."

She whipped her head back at that and he realized his mistake. "How do you know where we live?"

Shit. He was not getting into that. Him revealing how he was aware of her address when he had never set foot there—as far as she knew—would just add to the already mounting list of reasons for her to hate him.

"I must have heard it from Mami," he lied, but the words had an instant effect on Esme.

"Of course." Her eyes softened at the mention of his mother. "Gloria was able to visit before she got too weak."

When his mother had been losing her battle with cancer years earlier, Ivelisse had been there to help, sitting with his mother for days on end. And he'd heard from Marquito that Esmeralda had come to the wake for a few hours when he'd been called away to do something for Patricio. Because even at his mother's funeral he'd had to put the studio first.

"Mami misses her." Her voice was hoarse with real emotion, and seeing her hurt for his mother cracked something open in him. He never talked about his parents; he'd stopped even mentioning his father's name after he disappeared, leaving Rodrigo holding the bag for his reckless gambling. Then his mother had gotten sick. But if anyone knew what his mother had meant to him, it was Esmeralda.

His twenties were a blur, nothing but overwhelming stress and paralyzing fear that they would be destitute, that his mother would die because they could not get her decent care. But he'd done what he'd needed to. Kept his head down and made himself indispensable to Patricio Sambrano until he was pulling in an eight-figure salary before he was thirty. Ten years of gritting his teeth, and the only moments of real happiness had been with this woman who he barely knew how to talk to anymore.

The car came to a stop and when he looked out, he saw the front of her building. He'd only been here that one other time, but everything that had to do with Esmeralda was permanently etched in his memory.

"419 Riverside Drive," Manny announced, and without saying a word to him Esmeralda pushed the car door open. He ought to let this go, to drive off and go back to his obligations, but instead he got out of the car and went after her.

"You're not even going say goodbye to me, Esmeralda?" he growled, hot on her heels.

"Goodbye," she said as she made her way to the entrance of the building. She tapped in the code for the door and soon they were inside the small but well-appointed lobby of her building. He had no idea what he was doing, but he just could not let her go.

"You're being unreasonable. This is my life," he hissed as she walked into an alcove by the door.

She came to a dead stop as his angry words resounded in the space and spun on him so quickly they almost crashed into each other. "And this is *my life*, Rodrigo. I didn't ask to be Patricio's daughter or tell him to do what he did in his will. But I *am* shooting my shot." She laughed and it sounded broken. "I want this, Rodrigo. I have ambitions. Don't you think I wish things were different? I..." Her voice broke and she lifted her eyes to the ceiling, blinking fast. "I'm sorry this is the hand we've both been dealt. And I really thought that we could, that maybe—"

But whatever she was about to say died in the space between them. "You know what, never mind what I thought."

She turned again and walked over to the elevator as he stood there rooted to the floor. Unable to go after her, but not wanting to leave without fixing what was happening between them. He wanted to know what it was she wouldn't say. But as soon as the door opened their chance to talk was drowned out by a familiar cacophony of *holas* and *mijas*. And he was screwed, because Ivelisse Peña and her three sisters all came out of the elevator, a swarm of Dominican aunties heading straight for him.

"Niña, why didn't you tell me Rodrigo was coming over?" Esme's mother cried as she engulfed him in a hug. The top of her head barely reached his shoulder, but like his mother, what she lacked in stature she more than made up for in temperament.

She put her hands on either side of his face and he bent down so she could kiss him on the cheek. "Ivelisse, it's been a minute."

She clicked her tongue, pulling back so she could get a good look at him. "Too long." She patted him on the cheek and pursed her lips in a sad expression. "You got Gloria's face. Verdad?" she asked her sisters, who promptly gave him more hugs. He felt starved for touch. But even with these women loving on him he felt cold and bereft, because the only person he wanted, the only hands he yearned for, belonged to the woman who was standing off to the side looking miserable.

He took a step back as Ivelisse asked him questions about his brother. "Marquito's good. Loves his job," he said with a smile he was certain didn't reach his eyes. He was proud of his brother, but he couldn't get excited about anything in that moment. He needed to leave. Walking in here after Esmeralda had been a terrible idea. "Listen, Ive, it was good seeing you, but I have to get going. I just came to drop off Esme."

Ivelisse was a wily woman and the mere mention of her daughter's name seemed to wake up her spidey senses. Instantly her gaze was shifting back and forth between the two of them as if she was picking up a signal from inside their heads.

"I'm not letting you out of this building until you

come up and have a cafecito with us. Esmeralda, what are you doing standing there in a corner looking mad? Ven, mija." She waved over her only child, who indeed looked very unhappy to be in this tableau.

"I have my driver outside," Rodrigo pleaded, knowing Esme probably didn't want him anywhere near her.

But Ivelisse would not be dissuaded. "Rebeca, go tell the driver Rodrigo's going to come up for a visit."

And that's how he found himself sitting in Esmeralda's living room getting plied with coffee and Dominican pastries during the middle of a workday.

Fourteen

Esmeralda wanted the floor to open up and swallow her whole. Because she was pretty sure she reeked of sex and was now surrounded by her mother and all her aunts while they cooed over Rodrigo, who also probably reeked of sex. They were sitting on her mother's love seat while the older women ran around setting out food for the honored guest. Because God forbid a male visitor came to the house and they didn't serve him an elaborate feast like he was a freaking emperor.

"Esmeralda, mamita, what did those pastelitos ever do to you? Stop looking at my food like it offended you." Her mother thought she was cute. But if she didn't stop glaring Ivelisse would pick up on the fact that something was wrong. And her mother was not above asking her twenty questions in front of company.

"Sorry, Mami," she mumbled and leaned in to grab a cheese pastelito. She was annoyed but also hungry and the fried cheese-filled pastry would at least put her in a more amenable mood. When she leaned back into the couch, next to freaking Rodrigo, her hand accidentally grazed his thigh. His hard and very muscular thigh, which she'd been astride just an hour ago…before he reminded her again that he was not interested in anything other than pushing her out. She expected him to be put out, or bored, looking at his watch, desperate to leave their small apartment, but he appeared totally at ease with arms splayed over the back of the couch. He should feel out of place here in his five-thousand-dollar suit and expensive haircut. But somehow, he fit.

"I'm heading out soon," he said against her ear, and her body flooded with heat. "I just didn't want to be rude to Ive."

She exhaled and turned to him. "It's fine. It's not like they would've taken no for answer."

At that precise moment her mother walked out from their little kitchen carrying a tray laden with steaming cups of café con leche. Rodrigo sprung up from the couch as soon as he saw her, his arms extended to get the tray from her. "Ivelisse, you should've called me, I would've brought this out for you." Her mother waved him off, but happily handed him the heavy tray.

"You were always such a helpful boy." She leaned in to kiss him on the cheek as he handed cups to Esmeralda's aunts. Something about her mother's expression gave Esme pause. She looked regretful, like she always did whenever Rodrigo was in the picture.

"Rebeca, how's the teaching gig? Are you still up at Gregorio Luperón?" Esme's aunt perked up at Rodrigo's question about her beloved students. Esmeralda seriously resented the ball of warmth pulsing in her chest at the fact that he remembered the high school her aunt worked at.

"It's a roller coaster," Rebeca answered with a laugh. "Teaching those math kids that the arts are also important is always a struggle. But I keep trying."

"If anyone's going to get through to them it's you," he told Rebeca with a fond smile. By that point every one of the older women was riveted by him. And Esme couldn't blame them. The man was a walking, talking sex dream. Her hands twitched as that sculpted chest flashed in her mind. He was back to looking picture-perfect. Only an hour earlier she'd had her hands all over him. She'd kissed that generous mouth, nipped at his neck.

Yeah. She needed to calm down.

"I might be able to give you hope," Rodrigo said to Rebeca after taking a huge bite of pastelito. She really had to stop staring at his mouth. "My mentee just started his first year in the NYU film studies program and he went to Luperón."

"You still do that?" Esmeralda interrupted. "The Big Brother program, I mean." The words were out of her mouth before she could stop herself and soon four sets of eyes were on her.

Rodrigo turned his gaze to her and the intensity there was enough to make her fan herself. "Yeah, I do." He nodded, eyebrows furrowed.

"You've been in that mentoring program since college."

He dipped his head again. "Yeah, I actually started an initiative at Sambrano for people interested in being mentors. In the beginning it was just the New York offices, but it went so well we expanded it to Miami and LA, too. Altogether we have like two hundred mentors."

"That's wonderful, Rodrigo." Her mother had always been Rodrigo's number-one fan. The rest of the tías chimed in and soon he was asking each of them questions about their interests and jobs. He had them practically eating out of his hand. But that wasn't fair, either. This wasn't manipulative or fake. He cared about these women. He'd grown up around them. Because they had a history together. A history she'd forced herself to never think about—but that didn't mean it wasn't there.

And Esmeralda wished it felt like history, like something that was part of her past. But in just a matter of days Rodrigo had become a presence in her life she couldn't ignore, and worse—one she didn't know how to walk away from. Even when she was furious with him, she couldn't deny how right it felt to have him in her life. He was at home here. In her world, with her mother, with her aunts. Because he had always been a part of all of it.

"Where are all the Juanes and Keanu Reeves posters?" Rodrigo asked, eliciting a wry smile and nudge on his shoulder.

"I am a grown woman, Rodrigo. My teenage crushes are ancient history," she said, waving him over to the standing desk near the window. In reality her bedroom was sexy as hell. Dark blues and golds, a big inviting bed, and lots of art on the wall. Yeah, this was not a kid's room and the things he wanted to do to her on that bed were definitely for adults only.

"Come, let me show you something." For once Rodrigo was grateful for the diminutive spaces in New York City apartments. It gave him an excuse to get closer to her again. She'd thawed in the hour since they'd gotten to her apartment. And he couldn't deny that it had been nice to spend some time with Ivelisse and her sisters. He had to hold himself so tightly all the time at work that he forgot who he had been. Before everything had gone wrong with his parents, with Esmeralda, his life had not been only about garnering power at Sambrano. His life had been this, la familia.

Esmeralda had been the place where he always

felt grounded in that, but since they'd parted, he'd changed. He'd closed himself off; he'd told himself all he needed was the job. And now in less than three days her presence had started chiseling at that barrier he'd created between himself and the world. He could feel the walls of control crumbling with every kiss. And instead of retreating, of trying to find a way to get himself back to the safety of aloofness, all he wanted was to get closer. He had no idea how he'd do it, how he would manage to keep her and the job, but with every passing second he grew more certain that finding a way was the key to everything.

He tentatively moved closer, his front only inches from her back, and instead of pulling away from him she leaned in. Almost instinctively he wrapped an arm around her waist. He pressed his lips to her neck, flicking his tongue at the warm skin there.

"I'm supposed to be showing you something," she protested as her hand skittered off the keyboard. Within seconds she'd turned around in his arms.

He trailed kisses from her mouth all the way down to the top of her breasts, lapping at her skin as she gasped with pleasure. "I have no self-control at all with you," she moaned, and despite her mother and aunts being just down the hall, his hunger for her was too fierce to stop.

"Let me see you, Joya," he urged and she quickly obliged, revealing those gorgeous breasts for him. "Mmm, tweak them for me, show me where you want my hands, sweetheart." His hands itched to touch her, but this game of her pleasuring herself while he watched had always been a favorite of theirs.

She took his hand and guided it to an engorged peak. He worried the nipple between his thumb and index finger, and watched her gasp with pleasure. "I love seeing you like this." *I don't think I can live without it*, he almost said, but instead focused on what he had now. He moved in to kiss her and she responded with the same hunger he felt. Her tongue sliding with his, tasting and nipping until he almost regretted having started something he could not finish.

He pulled back, gasping "I need to have you again."

She nodded frantically, going in for another kiss. "I can't disappear on my mom tonight," she said regretfully. "But maybe tomorrow," she promised and a sound of pure pleasure rumbled in his chest.

"I would like that." He was about to go in for another kiss, to show her just how much he wanted her, when his phone went off. It was the ringtone he'd set for friends and family—which now were only a precious few. For it to be a call and not just a text meant it had to be urgent.

He pressed a soft kiss to her jaw and pulled back regretfully. "I'm sorry, I have to take this."

She nodded in understanding as she fixed her top. "We should stop anyway, my mother is already going to ask me a thousand questions, and I don't need to walk out there looking like you just had your way with me."

"Which I did," he teased, inciting a glare from her. A smile tugged at his lips as he tapped to accept a call from…Jimena?

"What's up?" he asked into the phone as Esmeralda gestured she was going back outside to rejoin her mother and aunts. She had barely closed the door behind her when Jimena launched into a frantic story about Carmelina.

"Slow down. I don't understand a single thing you're saying."

"Sorry," she said, sucking in a breath as if she'd just come up from being underwater. "I'm just freaking out."

He sighed, heart already galloping in his chest from whatever she was about to tell him. Jimena was the single most coolheaded person he knew. Hearing her admit she was freaking out surely meant something really bad was happening.

"Tell me."

"I just got an interesting call from one of my friends who works in the legal counsel office at Global Networks. Word is that Carmelina and her kids have a meeting with Burt Deringer tomorrow."

Rodrigo's hackles went up at the mention of the CEO of the company that had made a previous aggressive attempt to buy Sambrano. He knew Carmelina was callous, but selling out to Deringer was downright evil.

"She's selling him her shares," Jimena said, ominously. Damn the woman and her unstoppable greed. "Apparently Onyx and Perla's, too." He felt the surge of anger rise in him like a fireball. Deringer's previous bid to buy Sambrano was six years earlier, right after Rodrigo had taken over as chief content officer. The money they'd offered had been excessive, but when they presented their plans for the network, Patricio had backed out. They'd intended to gut the programming and take out all cultural nuance. They had no interest in preserving Sambrano's brand, they just wanted to own everything they could. And now, barely a year after her husband's death, Carmelina was looking to sell out to the absolute last people Patricio would have wanted in control. "How could she do this?"

"Because she's a money-hungry witch?"

"No, it's more than that. She'd rather see this place in ruins than let Esmeralda be the face of Sambrano. She hasn't wasted the chance to remind Esmeralda of that in the past few days. I really thought even if only to save face, she wouldn't sink to this, but I was wrong." He shook his head as he paced the small space between Esme's bed and her desk. The warm and easy feeling from just minutes earlier now transformed into sick dread.

Jimena sighed again, tongue clicking. "I can't believe Perla's going for this."

"She's nowhere near as bad as Onyx," Rodrigo agreed, "but she's always let Carmelina steamroll her." Patricio's youngest daughter was no match for her mother's malice. "There are still Esmeralda's shares, which she can't touch, but she technically doesn't need her to sell the rest."

"No, she's got the three votes." Jimena's voice was tight with worry as she confirmed what they both knew. Sambrano's only provision regarding selling shares to an outside party was that three out of the four majority shareholders agreed on the sale. As things stood right now, the shares were equally divided between Carmelina and Patricio's three children. With Onyx and Perla on their mother's side, Esme would not be able to stop her father's widow from essentially selling the company out from under her.

Rodrigo's fury rose as he surmised the repercussions of what Carmelina was planning. If she got her way she'd not only get rid of Esme, but would finally get him out of the picture, too. Anger burned in his gut like hot coals. Almost twenty years of this, of Carmelina scheming and destroying because of her fucked-up sense of entitlement over everything Patricio owned.

Esmeralda at least deserved the chance to have a say in the future of her father's company. That was something that had never been in question—even if he was determined to keep his job, he had never intended to see Esmeralda cast out. But if Carmelina did this, there was no saving Sambrano. He looked at the door and heard the women on the other side chattering happily and swore to himself he would do whatever it took to stop that woman from pushing Esmeralda out.

“Wait,” Jimena said, bringing him out of his thoughts. “I just got a really cryptic text from Magdalena. I told her about the meeting with Deringer and she’s been doing some digging around of her own.” The CFO from Sambrano was a straight shooter and if therc was anything amiss, she would find it.

“What did she say?” Rodrigo asked, his focus back on Jimena.

“She’s asking me to come to her place in an hour,” Jimena said, and Rodrigo could hear her fingers tapping on a keyboard. “She says she called in some favors and she’s got some information about Carmelina’s finances.”

Rodrigo had heard enough. He stormed out of the room after promising to meet Jimena at Magdalena’s penthouse in an hour. When he stepped into the living room he found Esme smiling as she chatted happily with her mother and aunts. He’d be damned if he let Carmelina try to break this woman again. “I have to go,” he told Esme, who stood up from where she’d been sitting with her mother when he appeared.

“Are you all right?” she asked, probably noticing the tension coming off of him in waves.

For a second he considered telling her. Maybe it would be good to let her know what was going on. But then he thought of the blow that would be. To know that Carmelina had not even considered playing fair. That her siblings were colluding with their mother to end Esme's chances.

He didn't want Carmelina's machinations to mess with Esmeralda more than they already had. Besides, he was still CEO of the company and it was his job to fix this, not Esme's. No matter how much he wished for them to be able to find a way to continue to spend time together—perhaps even more than that after this was all over—he had a job to do.

"I'm fine," he lied, as he leaned in to press a kiss to her cheek. "Something came up that I need to take care of. I'll see you at the office tomorrow."

She nodded slowly, her face doubtful. She could tell something was up, but she didn't pry. "Okay, I'm going to try to finish my presentation tonight. Would you be able to take a look at it in the morning?"

"Sure," he said distractedly, his mind already racing with all the things he needed to do. Hoping it would be enough to thwart Carmelina and her kids. "I'll look at it as soon as I get in." With that he did a round of kisses and apologies for having to take off, and within minutes he was back in the town car. His phone buzzed and his stomach clenched in response when he saw Carmelina Sambrano's name flashing on the screen.

"How could you do this?" he growled into the speaker before she got a chance to get a word in.

"Wow, Rodrigo, you actually do have the ability to emote?"

He breathed through his nose, trying to manage the consuming anger this woman was inciting in him. "Are you really going to throw away your husband's life work just so Esmeralda doesn't have a chance to be the CEO?"

"I'm not really interested in talking details over the phone, querido, but I do have an offer for you."

"Why would you think I'd ever agree to do anything with you?" he asked as rage tore through him.

"Because I can make sure you can keep your job—and more importantly, that fifty-million-dollar salary you're always saying you sacrificed so much to get."

There it was. He'd known she'd do this. She thought she finally had the thing that would lure him to her side. He felt his back molars grind together at the derision in her voice. Like he hadn't earned every fucking cent he made. Like it wasn't a fraction of the money he'd brought in for Sambrano over the years. "Deringer has agreed to keep you on as CEO *if* you help facilitate the negotiations. With your support behind the sale, the board will be more amenable."

All the blood rushed to his head at once and he felt like he was going to be sick. This woman really thought she could just buy him off. That he would betray Patricio, Esmeralda and himself for money.

Then again, Carmelina didn't understand loyalty; she didn't get what it was like to stand by something because you believed in it. She only believed in one thing: herself. She only cared about winning. And that's where he would beat her at her own game.

Fifteen

"Where the hell *is* he?" Esmeralda was trying not to panic. But it was now a full eighteen hours since Rodrigo had stormed out of her apartment and had stopped answering her texts.

She winced, remembering what they'd been up to right before whatever he saw on his phone caused him to take off without an explanation. After he'd left, she'd shut everything out and gotten to work. She'd used the files she'd gotten from Mr. Piera and worked all night on her presentation. She was pleased with what she'd come up with, confident this was a plan the board could get behind. It was bold and it was more ambitious than anything the studio had done in decades, but she believed it was the key to taking Sambrano into the future. Except she had no one to run it by, and Rodrigo was MIA. He'd promised her he'd be here today to give her feedback, but no one had seen or heard from him all morning.

Maybe he was ignoring her because he was going to let her go into that board meeting and fall on her face. Had she been a fool for thinking that the way he'd been with her mother and aunts meant something? That it would somehow change the fact that he was still hoping she failed? Her phone buzzed and her heart practically came up her throat, but it was just her meditation app reminding her to breathe. She took the excellent advice and focused on letting air in and out of her lungs, and tried to stay grounded in facts, not feelings. She was good at her job, she knew the market, she knew the industry. *She knew she was on to something.*

"I don't need Rodrigo to do this," she told herself for the hundredth time since she'd gotten in at 8:00 a.m. "I got this," she said now, feeling stronger.

"*Do you got this?* Because it looks to me like your nerves are getting the best of you." Esmeralda snapped her head up from the slides she'd been reviewing…again, to find Onyx standing in front of her. He looked just as mean as he had at the reception.

"Why are you here?" She didn't even try to hide her animosity.

He sneered at her and lifted a shoulder as if he had all the time in the world. "Oh, just came to check if Rodrigo gave you a heads-up about the meeting with the buyers."

"Buyers?" Even though she had no clue what that even meant, her heart still pounded in her chest, apprehension pooling in her stomach. "What are you talking about?" She didn't know her brother very well, but she did recognize a smug jackass when she saw one. Esmeralda had a feeling that whatever Onyx was here to tell her would almost certainly ruin her day.

"Oh, he didn't tell you? He's on his way to a meeting with Global Networks. They've made an offer to buy the studio. He's going there with my mother." Bile churned in her stomach as Onyx walked in a little closer, for the last piece of gossip he had to share. Esme braced for it. "They want him to stay on as CEO, so he's all in."

"You're lying," she said, even as her mind reeled.

"Am I?" Onyx asked, showing her rows of perfectly white teeth. "Has anyone even heard from him today?" He was speaking so casually, like they were just chatting about the weather. God, he was cruel. "Mr. Workaholic is usually at his desk at 7:00 a.m. sharp, but no one's heard from him since yesterday. Ask his assistant."

He was right.

All the wind went out of her lungs at once, the pain of Rodrigo's betrayal like a knife in her gut. But she would be damned if she let Onyx get the satisfaction of seeing her undone. She quickly regrouped and tried her best to send a withering look toward her brother. She gathered as much strength as she could, even as she reeled from the bomb that he'd had just detonated.

How could Rodrigo do this? Had he been in cahoots with Carmelina even as he told her that the woman was a snake? Even as he assured her again and again that he would not interfere with her presentation, that he wanted the CEO position only if he got it fair and square? But maybe that was the problem, that he thought Esmeralda didn't deserve it. Maybe the way he saw it was that she'd sauntered in and tried to claim the position unfairly. And she'd let him distract her with sex and her messiness. He was probably using her unprofessional behavior as an excuse to push her out at this very moment.

"Get out of my office, Onyx," she demanded. "Unlike you, I have work to do. If Rodrigo is scheming with your mother then good luck to him. Just two days ago she was telling him he was a nobody, and today she's doing business with him. Sounds like they deserve each other."

With that she turned her attention to the monitor in front of her in an attempt to ignore Onyx's ugly sneer.

"I'd start cleaning out my stuff if I were you," he said in an awful singsong voice.

"In case you forgot, I still own twenty-five percent of the shares in this company." To her surprise, the comment seemed to make him even more smug.

If that melodramatic laugh was anything to go by anyways.

"You're in for all kinds of surprises today," he gloated maliciously before rushing off.

Esmeralda felt a sob closing her throat, and she savagely pushed it down. She would be damned if anyone in this place saw her shed a single tear. She had vowed to never cry over Rodrigo Almanzar again. And she would not break that promise to herself today. Esme had really thought her heart was done breaking for that man.

She'd been so wrong.

He'd literally left her apartment, after kissing her mother and tías, to go meet with Carmelina Sambrano and concoct a way to push her out. She counted to fifty after Onyx was out of her office before she stood up and hurried to shut the door. Not that it gave her much privacy since all the office walls were made of glass, but at least no one would be able to hear her. She grabbed her phone and quickly dialed the only person she knew who would help her figure out what to do.

"Mami." She could barely choke the word out at the relief of hearing her mother's loving and familiar voice.

"Mija, what's wrong?"

Esmeralda let out a shaky breath, relief coursing through her. She could always count on her mother's unfailing steadiness. Even when nothing else worked, her mother was always there for her. Her rock, the person who always stood by her no matter what. For a time she'd believed that Rodrigo could be that for her, too. But he'd proven again and again that his only loyalties were to himself and to the Sambranos.

"I'm not sure what's going on, but Onyx was just here and told me that Rodrigo and Carmelina are meeting with an outside buyer. That he's working with her to stay on as CEO and get rid of me." Saying that last part out loud almost broke her. She could not believe she'd trusted him again. Was she so desperate for acceptance that she'd put herself in this position again with a man who had proven to her she was expendable to him? "I can't believe I let Rodrigo play me again."

She was pathetic.

"Esmeralda, take a breath, mi amor. What are you talking about? What happened?" Her mother's voice was taut with tension. She hated worrying Ivelisse, but this felt too familiar. Like those times when her mother had reluctantly let Esmeralda go spend time with her father only to see her return in tears after being humiliated by Carmelina's venomous words.

"Rodrigo's going to help Carmelina sell the studio so he can stay on as CEO."

Esme squeezed her eyes shut when she heard her mother's shocked gasp. "Ay, mija. Are you sure? I can't believe he would do that."

"He *is*, Mami," she cried, sick to her stomach with

regret. "I get that *she's* scheming against me, hell, I even expected it." She fought to keep her voice low. "But to know that Rodrigo is in on it with her… I should've known he hadn't changed." She scoffed, shaking her head as her belly roiled with nausea and uneasiness. "I don't even know why I'm surprised. He's done this to me before."

Esme heard her mother suck in a breath, as she sat there steeped in misery. For a moment she wondered if she should just leave. Grab her purse and her laptop and leave these people and their drama behind. "Maybe this is for the best. Maybe I just need to walk away from all this."

"Esmeralda, I'm going to tell you something right now and I need you to understand that I kept this from you because I thought it was for the best."

"Mami, what are you talking about?" Esmeralda had never heard her mother sounding so serious. Ivelisse Peña was one of those people who managed to maintain a positive outlook even in the darkest of moments, but right now she sounded subdued. Scared even, and that, more than anything that had occurred in the past hour, terrified Esmeralda.

"I need to tell you the truth about the reason why your father evicted us from that apartment and why Rodrigo disappeared on you that weekend."

Esmeralda felt the skin on her face tighten at her mother's words, sickening dread roiling in her gut. "He left you because his mother called him and told him what Patricio was doing and he jumped on a plane to come help me."

"What?" Esmeralda's voice sounded distant to her own ears, like she was speaking from somewhere far away. "Why didn't he tell me that, Mami?"

"He was so careful back then, Esmeralda. He had so much to lose." Ivelisse sighed tiredly. "I still don't know how he managed, but within twenty-four hours that boy found me this apartment, figured out the down payment and had movers coming to the house to pack me up and take our stuff the two blocks down from our old place." Her mother clicked her tongue, a sound Esme knew she made only when she was thinking hard. "I swore I would never tell you this, but I think it's important for you to know what you're up against there.

"Your father sent me that eviction notice after Carmelina showed him a fake paternity test. One that said you weren't his." Her mother's voice broke as Esmeralda sat there in stunned silence. She knew Carmelina was vicious, but this was monstrous.

"She did what!" she shouted on the phone, hardly able to believe what she was hearing.

"She forged a paternity test," her mother said numbly. "That was after Patricio agreed to pay for your master's at NYU. She knew you were getting an education that could put you in a position to take over the company someday, and like the vicious bitch she is, she tried to sabotage you." Esme sank into one of the armchairs in the office, reeling from what her mother had just told her.

"I don't even understand. My father just took her word for it?" She was fighting to get the words out at this point.

"I'm not going to make up excuses for Patricio, because he should've known better, but apparently she had papers. Rodrigo was the one who discovered she'd faked it all." And there went her heart, trying to gallop out of her chest again. "I still don't know how he figured it all out. He dug around and discovered the laboratories that supposedly ran the test didn't exist. And your father, who hated nothing more than looking foolish, was furious with Carmelina." Ivelisse laughed bitterly at that. "He was mad at everybody. He did walk back the eviction, though. But by then Rodrigo had helped me get into this building and that was that." Esmeralda heard another long and heavy sigh, as she tried to process what her mother had just told her.

"Mija, Rodrigo ensured Carmelina could never pull something like that again. That boy stood up to your father, and risked losing his job to make sure your place as Patricio's daughter was never questioned again. Rodrigo's not perfect, but I don't believe the man who did that for us could ever betray you like that. And especially not with that woman."

Esmeralda felt like she was floating, her mind almost unable to take in everything she'd learned in the past five minutes. The resentment and the hurt she'd held on to for ten years had been based on a lie. Rodrigo had not been on her father's side, he'd been helping her mother. He'd been looking out for her.

"Why did no one tell me? Why did he break up with me?" she asked, a real sob escaping her lips.

Her mother sighed. "He begged me not to tell you he helped, and about the break-up, I don't know, honey. He was in such a tough spot. You have to remember he was just starting to get ahead at the studio. He was fresh out of graduate school, had loans. His mother was sick and Patricio was still helping him get out from under all the debt that bum Arturo had racked up. Who knows what all went down between the two of them? Patricio was not a man to take people standing up to him well, and he would've seen Rodrigo dating you behind his back and helping me as an affront. Maybe he distanced himself from you to appease your father. I just don't know."

"Even if that's true, why didn't he tell me? It would've hurt to lose him, but at least I would've understood!"

Her mother made a comforting sound. "It will be all right, mija. I know you two will figure this out."

She was openly crying now, her mind like a tornado, thoughts swirling so fast she felt light-headed. "I have to figure out what's going on then. I have to find Rodrigo." Esmeralda felt numb, like her emotions had shut down.

"I think that's a good idea. And remember, sweetheart, you have a right to be there and you have people on your side. Never forget that."

She felt completely alone in that building, like there wasn't a single person on her side, but hearing her mother's words was a small comfort. A call came in right as she was about say goodbye and when she looked at the screen she frowned at the unknown number. "Someone's calling me, Mami."

"Call me as soon as you hear something." After promising she would, she picked up the other line.

"Esmeralda Sambrano-Peña," she said briskly.

"Talk to Jimena Cuevas." The voice on the phone sounded female, but they were obviously trying to muffle it to avoid being recognized.

"Who is this?" Esme asked tersely. "Why do I need to talk to Jimena?"

"She'll tell you what you need to know," the muffled voice said, but offered nothing else.

"Please, who am I talking to?" she asked urgently, but after a few seconds she realized there was no one on the other end. Without pausing to consider if this was just someone else trying to mess with her, she took the elevator to the legal counsel's office. Jimena's executive assistant tried to stop her, but Esmeralda barreled right into the woman's office.

"Esmeralda." If Jimena was surprised to see Esme crashing into her office unannounced, she did not show it. "Come in, please." Her tone was friendly, and she almost seemed glad to see her. Esme would just add it to the growing list of bizarre occurrences of the day.

"Do you know where Rodrigo is right now?"

"Close the door," Jimena said. This time her tone was more serious.

Once Esme did, she launched right into it. "Rodrigo's trying to stop Carmelina from selling her and her children's shares to an outside party."

"Stopping? But Onyx said—"

Jimena shook her head, her mouth twisting sourly at the mention of Esme's sibling. "Rodrigo had to make them think he was in on it. They're meeting with the buyers in less than an hour at the Peninsula. Hopefully Rodrigo will have what he needs to stop her in time.

"Here," she said, jotting something on a sticky note and handed it to Esme. "They're meeting in this conference room."

"I'm going over there."

"Good," Jimena said approvingly. "I'll have my assistant arrange a car for you,"

Esmeralda shook her head. "It's only a few blocks from here, it'll take longer to drive. Besides, it'll give me a chance to calm down."

Rodrigo's friend canted her head to the side, as if she were only now really looking at Esmeralda. "You have guts, but you're not a hothead," she stated, approval in her voice. "You'll be good for him."

Esme was not going to answer that, and made a

move to walk out, but Jimena's voice stopped her. "He'll be pissed I told you, but it's about time Rodrigo learned he can't do everything on his own."

Sixteen

"I knew you'd come. I told that girl you're only loyal to yourself."

Rodrigo took one deep breath and then another as he walked into the small conference room Carmelina had arranged to sell out her husband's legacy. He looked at her and could barely keep the bile from rising in his throat. Carmelina had been a beautiful woman when she was young, with her pale skin and striking blue eyes. But she had not aged gracefully. Her face was twisted and swollen from too many procedures. She wore one of her signature Chanel suits in a navy blue with cream on the neck and cuffs. It was expensive and elegant, but on her it looked shabby, ill-fitting.

"So you've taken it upon yourself to sell the studio," he stated, barely able to contain his anger.

"Yes, I have." She looked smug as hell sitting at the head of the conference room table waiting for him. She really thought she had him. After years of trying to manipulate him, she thought she'd managed to find the one thing he would betray Sambrano over. But that had always been Carmelina's problem—she was too self-interested to ever notice that not everyone was motivated by the same things she was. She'd invited him here thinking she had him in her clutches. She had no idea how badly she'd miscalculated.

"You didn't think it was appropriate to consult the board on your plan to sell three-quarters of the company out from under them?" he asked, too incensed at this woman to not demand answers.

Carmelina lifted a shoulder as she poured packet after packet of sweetener into her iced tea. "I don't need to consult the board. All I needed was three out of the four majority shareholders on board. I have that," she said triumphantly. She smiled that cutting, menacing smile and a wave of disgust ran down Rodrigo's spine. "This isn't about money. This is about preserving the respectability of our name."

"Stop, Carmelina. We both know what this is about—spite and money. You can't get rid of Esmeralda, so you'd rather see Patricio's company destroyed." He didn't know if he was expecting remorse or even a flicker of emotion, but it was like talking to a wall.

"I guess you *are* smarter than you look, Rodrigo."

He ignored the jab as he fought for control. "Do you not care at all about the ramifications of this?"

"The only thing I care about is making sure I never have to hear or see that girl's name again."

He couldn't take it anymore. "Esmeralda being a part of the studio was Patricio's decision. It was his final wish, for goodness sake. Are you so dead inside that you don't care about your husband's legacy?"

"Patricio was always too sentimental. I'm the only one who's willing to do what's necessary. This is for the best." That's how Carmelina had done it all these years. The woman was so good at persuading people because the truth wasn't even a concept to her. She sounded convincing because to her, if she said it, *it was* the truth.

She looked Rodrigo up and down, her eyes roaming from his face all the way to his shoes, and the expression on her face told him that as always she found him thoroughly lacking. "But that's something someone like you would never understand."

Ten, hell, even five years ago those words would've stung. The reminder of his family's shame, of what his father had done slicing across his pride. Because she was right—there were not enough Brioni or Zegna suits in the world to cover up the fact that if it wasn't for Patricio's help his family would've ended up on the street. But he was not ashamed of who he was, and his conscience was clean. He'd never taken advantage of anyone to get to where he was. And now he had amassed enough wealth to never have to worry about money again. Rodrigo knew exactly what it took to stay on top when everyone around you wanted to see you fall. And what Carmelina didn't know was that he was about to beat her at her own game.

"That must be Deringer and his people." Carmelina jumped to her feet as the door opened. "And try not to look like you're about to go to the gallows, Rodrigo, would you?"

In that moment three men walked into the room—one he recognized as Deringer, the other men he assumed were his attorneys. Deringer's face was constantly all over the news. The online retail magnate who had turned his interests to television and film, and in the past few years had amassed multiple networks, streaming services and film studios. The disturbing part was that he seemed to transform the programming into nothing but advertisements for his other companies. If Deringer acquired Sambrano he would turn it into a whitewashed Spanish language infomercial.

"Gentlemen, come in," Carmelina crowed, all smiles. The introductions were being made when a harried Onyx walked into the room.

"Ah, my children are here, we can finally get started." The frown on the younger man's face and the worry lines bracketing his mouth were a sharp contrast to Carmelina's overly genial tone. Carmelina kept her eyes on the door to the conference room while Onyx whispered in her ear, as if waiting for someone else to walk in.

Rodrigo smiled to himself, well aware of what was coming. He caught the exact moment she understood what was unfolding. Her shoulders stiffened and her mouth twisted into a snarl. He could tell she was battling to control herself. That she didn't want Deringer to figure out there was a problem. And Rodrigo went in for the kill.

"Perla's not coming, Carmelina," he said in her same sickly sweet tone. She pivoted her head up, looking at him suspiciously.

"Of course she is," she snapped, and then stopped herself, probably remembering she had an audience.

"Is there an issue?" asked one of the two men flanking Deringer. The magnate had not looked up from whatever he was doing on his phone, seemingly only there to sign the paperwork and go on with his day. The fact that Carmelina was willing to hand over everything her husband had worked so hard for to someone who only saw it as another pawn in his chessboard galvanized Rodrigo's anger.

"Just a little hiccup with my daughter. But we'll get her over here right away," Carmelina assured the man as Onyx looked at his mother with a terrified expression.

"Oh, I'd say there's more than a little hiccup," Rodrigo told her. "You no longer have seventy-five percent of the shares to sell."

Carmelina laughed hysterically, her eyes wide as she rushed to talk over Rodrigo. "What are you talking about? My children and I are ready to sell to Global Networks. We have three out of four votes as majority shareholders."

"No, you don't," Rodrigo corrected her as he pulled out the papers from his briefcase. "This morning Perla sold me her shares, and thus her vote, for the sum of two hundred million dollars." Liquidating practically everything he owned, calling in every favor he'd garnered over the past sixteen years, was worth getting to see the realization dawn on Carmelina's face that he'd beaten her at her own game. "You don't have the votes to sell anything to Global Networks," he told her, eliciting a scream of absolute fury.

"You can't do this! You're nobody, you're a paid employee. This company belongs to my children!" She looked at Deringer, who was already standing up and packing up his stuff as if he was about to walk out of the room.

Rodrigo held up a hand to stop her lies. "You're selling the company because you're broke. Your father's investments in the last ten years have completely depleted your family's fortune, and you've been funneling all of Patricio's money to keep him afloat. And now you're going to sell what's left to keep sinking money into a bottomless pit."

The door burst open again and Esmeralda walked in with Octavio Nuñez, both of them looking like they were walking into battle. And even if her arrival would only make Carmelina even more vicious, he was glad to see her.

"You, this is all your fault." Carmelina lunged for Esme as Deringer and his people stood up, clearly done with the Sambrano drama. "I won't let you take what belongs to me. I won't let you have it! I'd rather sell the studio for parts than let you win. Patricio was only too happy to believe that gold digger when she told him she was pregnant with his brat. I can prove you're not Patricio's child," she screamed frantically, rifling through papers, and he was ready for this, too.

"Stop lying, Carmelina. It's over!" Rodrigo roared as he got between Carmelina and Esmeralda. "Here." He handed the other piece of paper he'd brought with him to one of Deringer's attorneys. "This is an affidavit signed by Patricio Sambrano confirming that he is in fact Esmeralda's father."

He felt Esmeralda's legs give out, but he held her up, as he tried to end this farce with Carmelina once and for all.

"I got you," he told her, but she seemed too shocked to react. He looked over at his mentor's widow, who was now frozen in place, her eyes darting between Rodrigo and Deringer. "You're done, Carmelina."

Seventeen

"What are you doing here?" Rodrigo asked Esmeralda as they made their way out of the room, with Carmelina's shrieks trailing behind them.

"I'm here because this also concerns me, Rodrigo." Esme looked heartbroken, like all of this was beyond what she could bear. "I had a right to know Carmelina was working behind the board's back to sell the company from under me. From under all of us."

He wanted to reach out to her, but he didn't know how she'd react to that. She looked furious and hurt. Octavio came up to them, his expression bleak. "I wish you would've let us know what was happening, Rodrigo, but we're grateful that you put a stop to this. My cousin has always been like this, selfish enough to destroy everything to get what she wants." He shook his head, and it seemed like overnight Octavio had aged a decade. "We're calling an emergency meeting for the day after tomorrow." Octavio turned to Esmeralda then. "I'm sorry to do this, but we'll have to cut your preparation time. You will have to present then." Her face fell, but soon she was nodding.

"I can do that. I'll be ready." His chest swelled with love for her in that moment. His Joya. So strong, always ready to fight, never giving up on her dreams.

"Thank you for understanding and thank you for alerting me to what was going on." Octavio looked at Rodrigo as he spoke. He could see the man was not happy to have been kept in the dark, but Rodrigo had no regrets. If he hadn't talked Perla into selling him the shares without giving Carmelina warning that he was working against her, she would've pulled rank with her younger daughter. At this very moment Carmelina would have been destroying the company.

"Needless to say the board has a lot to consider right now given what has happened." Octavio's gaze was fixed on the door to the conference room where presumably Carmelina was still in a rage. But after a moment the man grinned at Rodrigo, clearly curious. "How did you manage to get Perla to sell you the shares?"

Rodrigo lifted a shoulder and glanced at Esme, who seemed to be waiting for Octavio to be done with him, so she could give him a piece of her mind. It seemed like the initial shock of walking in on Carmelina's fiasco had worn off and she did not seem happy with him at all.

Octavio cleared his throat, still waiting for an answer from Rodrigo, and he did his best to focus. "Perla doesn't trust her mother as much as people thought. A few years ago I helped her hire a financial advisor who was independent from the family. When he told her Carmelina had been trying to gain access to her trust fund, Perla had finally had enough of the scheming. She wanted out." This he directed at Esme. "She's never been keen on the games her mother plays. She's not like Onyx."

"Good for Perla and for you," Octavio said, and with a quick goodbye headed toward the exit of the hotel.

That only left him and Esmeralda.

"I hope you're happy," she said, her arms crossed over her chest. And once again his body reacted in about fifteen conflicting ways to Esmeralda's presence. His heart pounded and his body pulsed with the need to have her against the nearest flat surface, and then take her somewhere he could keep her safe and far away from the likes of Carmelina Sambrano.

"Why are you mad at me? I thought you'd be glad to hear that Carmelina no longer has control of the company." I thought you'd be glad I was able to help you, he almost said. She had to know he'd saved her chance at becoming CEO.

Without saying a word she turned on her heels and walked toward a small room beyond the larger one they'd just exited. He followed her in silence, certain that whatever he was walking into, it would not be pleasant. Once they were inside the room, she turned to face him. Her eyes were furious.

"Why could you let me think for *ten years* that you chose my father over me? How could you, Rodrigo?" He stumbled as what she said sank in. *She knew.*

"Ivelisse was not supposed to say anything." He exclaimed, his mind and body in absolute turmoil. "You were never supposed to know. I was trying to keep you safe. To protect you from all these filthy lies and schemes." He looked up at her and he could tell she saw the brokenness in his eyes, but he didn't have the energy to hide it anymore.

"You really let me believe all this time that when I needed you most you chose *him*? That I wasn't worth anything to you?" She shook her head as tears streamed down her face. God, he had made such a mess of everything.

"I had no choice, Esmeralda," he spat out, now his own anger and resentment coming to the surface. "I'm always the one to fall on the sword. The one to do what needs to be done and then get scorned for making the hard choices. Like everyone else you chose to believe that I'm a cold, selfish bastard."

She flinched at his words, but she regrouped quickly and soon she was on him again. "Maybe we all assume that because you give us nothing, Rodrigo. You love to be the martyr. Acting like no one cares about you. Like it's Rodrigo Almanzar against the world. Maybe people judge you because none of us really *know you*. Because you keep everything so tightly locked inside we can't get close enough. Because you never let anyone in."

"I let *you* in," he said in a voice he could barely recognize.

A sob escaped Esmeralda's throat at his words and when he reached for her she came to him. He pressed his mouth to hers in a frantic kiss. He felt like he was grasping at the last chance he'd ever have to touch her. She opened for him, like she needed him as desperately as he did her. Teeth scraping, hands grabbing, nails scratching. As if they were snatching the last bits of each other they'd get before they lost it forever. But after another moment she pushed him away.

"No." She shook her head. "I can't. I've been doing this all week. Letting my feelings make me forget how hard it was to lose you. How much it hurt to know my love for you wasn't enough. That it won't ever be enough."

"Esmeralda." It was on the tip of his tongue to say. He needed to say it. "I love you."

She squeezed her eyes shut like she couldn't bear to hear the words at all. "Don't say that. Don't tell me that when you hid the truth from me. When you don't treat me as your equal. Love is not just desire and lust, it's trust, it's a partnership, Rodrigo. My father spent years telling my mother he loved her and when it came down to it, he let her find out he married someone else on the news. Turned his back on her without even so much as an explanation." She swiped at her cheeks where tears were streaming down. "You say you love me, and yet in the past twenty-four hours you let me stay in the dark about a situation that had everything to do with me. That could determine my future." The raw pain in her voice, knowing he was responsible for putting it there, felt like someone was twisting a knife in his chest.

"I didn't want to worry you. Carmelina's a viper and she has no scruples. I wanted to spare you having to deal with her."

She laughed bitterly. "You think I don't know who Carmelina is, Rodrigo? That woman refused to let me come see my father when he was dying in the hospital. If you hadn't made sure my mother heard about it when he passed away, I would've found out he died from an obituary." She looked and sounded exhausted, bone tired.

"I'm not a child, Rodrigo. Do you know why I decided to claim the CEO position?" she asked, and he straightened, dread sitting in his stomach like lead. "It's true that I wanted to claim my place. That I wanted a chance to create my vision. But I also wanted to take something from you."

It hurt to hear it, but in a way he understood. Her

face was streaked with tears, misery rolling off her in waves. "I was so hurt. The two men in my life always choosing their damned corner offices over me. So, yeah, I wanted to take it from you."

She sounded small and wounded, and even as her words poked holes in his chest, he ached for her. "My father and his dysfunction, his games, turned everyone in his life into pawns. All of us wondering how we were lacking. Trying to blindly fix ourselves to deserve his love and his regard." Her words almost knocked him to the ground. Because she was right. "But now I realize that he had nothing to give. My father's only love was Sambrano. The thing he built, which in the end he couldn't care for, either. And I'm done thinking there was something in me that wasn't enough. I'm more than enough, and I deserve someone who sees that," she said, pressing a palm to her chest. "I deserve someone who sees me as an equal and continuing to expect it from people who can't give it to me is going to destroy me."

"This job is all I have, Esmeralda," he ground out, even as he saw the last bit of light go out of her eyes.

"Someday you'll figure out that's a lie you've been telling yourself. Too bad that when you do, you'll have pushed everyone who loves you away." And with that she walked out on him without a backward glance.

Eighteen

"Did you really think I was just going to let you get away with ignoring my calls?" Marquito asked as he pushed into Rodrigo's office. He'd gone home after the fallout with Esmeralda and had ignored everyone who'd tried to reach out to him. He was wrecked and at a loss of what to do, because she was right about everything.

He'd hoped to figure out how to talk to her, but tell her what? That they could make it work, even as he intended to take the job she was fighting for? He had no clue, but he could not deny the unbearable hollowness he'd been feeling since the moment she'd walked away from him.

And now here he was two days later, still at a loss on how to fix any of it.

"I'm not in the mood, little brother. The meeting with the board is in two hours and I still have no idea what's going to happen. And no matter what, there's no winning. Either I keep the job and she hates me or she gets it and I have to start over."

Marquito made a dismissive sound, which only made Rodrigo's mood darken further. "Starting over owning twenty-five percent of Sambrano is not exactly a bad place, and the board will never let you go. You know that. You own a quarter of this company now, Rodrigo," Marquito said, spreading his arms in the air. "Let that sink in. You had the means and the resources to come up with two hundred million dollars in *a day*. You have a stake in this place. You're no longer an employee, you're part owner of this studio."

He heard the words and still he felt nothing. He'd finally found a way to push out Carmelina, to defuse her power over the future of Sambrano, but he couldn't even enjoy it. Because in the process he'd ruined everything with the woman he loved. He could say that now. He would not hide from the truth now, and his love for Esmeralda was the greatest truth of his life. Just because he'd forced himself to ignore it for ten years didn't make it less of an undeniable fact.

"Esme knows about what went down with her mom ten years ago." Rodrigo knew he sounded wrung out, but there was no helping it. He was really at his wit's end.

"Shit." Marquito whistled. He'd been away at college when all that went down, but over the years his mom had talked about it. "I assume she didn't take it well."

He laughed bitterly at his little brother's understatement and he got up to get a bottle of water from the mini fridge in his office. "You could say that. She accused me of not trusting her, then when I told her I loved her she yelled at me some more. *Then* she told me I didn't treat her as an equal and was going to die alone."

He knew he was being unfair, that it was a hell of a lot more than that, but he was hurt. He felt once again that trying to do the right thing had cost him everything.

"She told me I had a martyr complex," he muttered, then snapped his head up when Marquito choked on the coffee he was drinking.

"You agree with that?" His little brother's cheeks flushed red at the question.

"I mean, she's not *totally* wrong." Marquito at least had the decency of sounding contrite.

"Of course she's not. What *she* are we talking about again?" Jimena's voice resounded in the office as she strode in. Figured that he would have everyone in Manhattan still talking to him here to hand him his ass at his lowest moment.

His brother, the traitor, grinned at his friend's arrival and lifted his coffee cup in Rodrigo's direction. "Esmeralda seems to have regaled my brother with some hard truths before telling him to get his shit together."

"Ah," Jimena responded in a tone that sounded very much like *it was about damn time someone did.*

He ought to throw them both out of his office, but they were the *only* two people left in his corner. "Are you two here to help me or pour salt on my wounds?"

"Did you hear the same thing I heard, Marquito?" Jimena asked, clutching her chest dramatically. "Did Mr. Lobo Solitario just utter the *H*-word?" She actually stage whispered, but he didn't think either of them were funny.

"I ask for help, dammit," Rodrigo said through clenched teeth. "You two think this is a joke? The woman I love thinks I would choose a job over her. Everyone in my life thinks I'm some kind of selfish, power-hungry drone. And I don't even know what all of this has been for," he said, looking out the window that gave him a clear view of Central Park and beyond. One of the most coveted views on earth, and looking at it right now, he felt empty.

"Maybe Carmelina was right, and I did sell my soul for this." He thought of the renovated brownstone that had costs millions, the ranch in Santa Fe with acres of land he'd never even been to, the villa in Punta Cana he rarely ever got to anymore. Money and properties that at one time seemed unattainable. He had so much now. But did he really enjoy any of it? He knew he wouldn't like the answer if he asked it out loud.

"Carmelina is never right," Jimena stated tersely as Marquito nodded in agreement.

But wasn't she? All he did was work and try to prove again and again that he deserved to be where he was. No personal life to speak of. And it *had* made him bitter. It had made him closed off, cold. After Esmeralda and then his mother, he had shut down. Until she'd walked back into his life a week ago and made him question everything.

"Rodrigo, for sixteen years you operated in the shadow of a brilliant but deeply flawed man, who cared for you, yes, but who also tended to treat the people he loved like shit." Jimena's voice was soft, like she didn't want to hurt him, but her gaze didn't waver from his. And he knew he had to hear this. "Which means, one, you need a really good therapist ASAP and two, you have to figure out what it is that *you* want, because news flash, you can do that now. You can walk out of here this minute and you will be doing it as a very wealthy man with a résumé and skill set only a few dozen people on the planet have. I can think of at least five networks who would ask you to name your price if it got out that you're a free agent."

"It's not that simple," he told Jimena, even as her words buzzed in his head.

"It is, though. You, my friend, have arrived at a place in your life where professionally and financially you not only have nothing to worry about, you have *choices*." He knew she was right. But the truth was he didn't want to leave Sambrano. His loyalty to this place was about more than just getting the corner office or the three letters after his name.

"I want to stay at Sambrano. This is finally my moment. After all this time I'm poised to do what I've always wanted to do with the studio." He thought of that old memo Esmeralda had found, the ideas he'd had and never been able to see come to fruition. He thought about the way Esme had clearly gotten his message. How she'd taken the seed of his idea and turned it into a vision for the future of Sambrano. They worked well together. They would make a hell of a team. "I have projects I want to see through. I have things I need to do. *I want to stay.*"

He loved the work he did here. He couldn't let go of the possibility of what the future could hold with him at the helm…and maybe, *maybe* with Esmeralda there, too.

"And what else do you want?" Marquito asked, with a knowing grin on his face.

"I want her by my side." He didn't need to tell them who, they both knew.

"Then go get her, pendejo," Jimena scolded him. "And don't just decide on what you think is a great idea and roll with it without letting her in on it like a jackass. That's what keeps getting you into messes."

"You're really taking advantage of the fact that I'm at a low moment to get all your digs in, aren't you?" he told his friend, who responded with a smart-ass grin. But a plan was already forming in his head. His heart leaped with the possibilities and he smiled as a thought started to form. He might have a solution for how Esmeralda and he could both be at the helm of Sambrano. He just had to convince her that they were better together than they were apart, in business *and* in love.

"Mija, are you hiding from me?" Ivelisse asked Esmeralda as she was sneaking around at the crack of dawn, trying to get out of the apartment before her mother woke up.

"No, Mami," she lied as she leaned in to kiss her mother on the cheek.

"I waited up for you until almost midnight."

"I was just going over my presentation, with the board meeting getting moved up and everything…" she trailed off as her mother studied her, aware that there was a lot more to her late night at the office than the presentation.

"You never told me how things ended. Just a text saying Rodrigo wasn't trying to push you out, and that you were fine. And you were MIA all day yesterday." Her mother reached up to tug gently on the thin hoops Esmeralda was wearing on her ears. The ones made of intertwined rose, yellow and white gold that she always wore for good luck. The ones that Rodrigo had given her for her twenty-first birthday.

"Tell me, mija."

"Rodrigo and I sort of started..." What could she even say? Hooking up like horny teens? That she'd told him she loved him and he'd said it back and then she'd walked out on him?

Her mother's soft laughter brought her out of her highly embarrassing thoughts. "Ay, Mija, even if I hadn't already suspected after you snuck in here almost at dawn after that cocktail party, I would've confirmed it the day he was here." Her mother's smile said *you're an adorable mess*. "You two have always been very bad at hiding the way you feel about each other."

"Well, it's over," she said miserably. She'd left that horrible meeting with Rodrigo and gone straight to her little office share. Had stayed there as much as she could since then. She could've gone home, but she didn't have it in her to answer questions from her mother. And she just could not face anyone at Sambrano. Not after the mess with Carmelina. Especially not when they'd moved her presentation up.

But she was ready, in part thanks to Rodrigo. The footage he'd given her access to and that memo of his she'd found had sparked the idea for her plan, but the conversations they'd had this week had cemented it. Despite the many challenges and disappointments he'd had in his time at Sambrano, Rodrigo still believed in the company. He believed in the mission. And Esmeralda found that she believed in it, too. She could clearly envision a path forward and she hoped she could be a part of making it happen.

And then there were her very complicated feelings for the acting CEO of Sambrano Studios.

It had been almost impossible to walk away from him after he uttered those words she never thought she'd hear again. But Rodrigo could not untangle his sense of obligation and misguided loyalties to her father from what he felt for her. She loved him, but she would not be with a man who could not be vulnerable. A man who didn't trust her, who didn't treat her like an equal partner. She deserved someone who could see in her the person who complemented them, who thought of her as essential to their life.

Her father had turned his back on her because she didn't fit into the image of the family he wanted to show the world. Rodrigo had walked away from her because he'd been ensnared by terrible choices. And even if she understood his reasons now, he could've told her the truth. He could've trusted that she was strong enough to bear it. But instead, he'd pushed her out of his life.

That was her, the person who never quite fit. The easiest one to crop out. The one whose absence wouldn't alter the outcome. And she was done with that. She wanted someone to whom she was essential, someone who not only saw her as part of the picture, but who believed there was no picture without her. She deserved that.

"Of course it isn't over." Her mother's voice pulled her back from her musings, and Esme had to smile at her determined expression. "You two are crazy about each other." Her mother clicked her tongue and pulled her by the hand to the corner of the apartment that held their kitchen. "Ven, te preparé un desayunito."

"Mami, I don't have time for breakfast. I need to get this presentation perfect. These people are just looking for an excuse to push me out. I'm not going to give it to them by showing up late."

"You have to eat, Esmeralda," her mother declared as she puttered around. "And you have to stop this thinking like you don't already belong there. Your father—"

Her mother closed her eyes, trailing off from what she was about to say. Esme had always wondered what her mother thought of whenever she recalled her relationship with Patricio. They'd been together for almost five years when he left her for Carmelina and in the years since, her mother rarely mentioned her time with him. It was like Esmeralda and that Cartier watch were the only proof there had been anything between her mother and Patricio Sambrano. Esme couldn't even recall ever seeing them in the same room together. When her father was done with Ivelisse it was like she'd ceased to exist. Esmeralda had never been able to wrap her head around how she'd coped with that kind of rejection. And still her mother had maintained her goodness, and raised her in a home full of love and optimism.

"Your father..." Her mother's voice cracked like thunder in their quiet kitchen. "Was a man who never learned to love himself. Even with all he achieved. Patricio built an empire from nothing. His mind was a marvel, so fearless, a real visionary. You remind me of him in that way." Her mother's smile was bittersweet. She focused on the window that gave them a view of the river, her eyes fixed on something in the distance. "But he never could shake off the demons of his past. He never let anyone get close enough. Not me, not his wife, his kids. He was so afraid of losing what he had, he never let himself enjoy it. But that has nothing to do with you and the right you have to be there. Patricio made so many mistakes in his life, but I think what he did with his will was his way of trying to make amends."

Esme shook her head at that. "Except he put me and Rodrigo at odds, and how fair was that for either of us?"

"It forced you to be together," Ivelisse quipped, and Esmeralda had to take a moment to think that bit through. "Patricio could be a real jerk, cruel even. But he rarely ever made missteps with his business."

"I don't know how this is going to end, Mami," Esmeralda confessed.

"You already belong in that boardroom. You're a Sambrano. Whether they agree or not. You have the means now to forge your own way, mija. If you don't want the shares, sell them. Start your own company. But if you want to stay, don't let anyone take that from you."

Her mother's words buoyed her, but still there was

Rodrigo. Her pushing for what she wanted would hurt him, and she hated that her father had put them in this situation. "Me getting the CEO position will oust Rodrigo." That didn't mean he couldn't stay on, but she didn't think he'd want to if it wasn't as CEO.

"That's something you both need to figure out together, how to forge forward."

"I told him it was over."

"Then go back in there and tell him you were wrong," her mother said as she brought her in for a hug. "Tell him you were scared. Tell him you want to try again. Rodrigo's not your father, baby. He's not perfect," Ivelisse conceded. "But that boy is loyal and he doesn't give up on the people he loves. Maybe what he needs to hear is that you'll be there for him, too. But first, breakfast."

Esme sat down with her bowl of oats fragrant with the cinnamon and lime zest her mother put in the milk and decided to maybe take her advice.

Nineteen

"I need to talk to you," they both said in unison when Rodrigo rushed into Esmeralda's office. He'd been waiting for her to get in for almost an hour, practically bursting with anticipation. The meeting with the board was set for noon and since his conversation with Jimena and Marquito he'd done nothing but work out the details of how to keep his job *and* the woman he loved. It was now 11:00 a.m., an hour before both their fates would be decided, and he was pretty certain he'd found the solution.

But of course, the moment he walked into her office, Esme had yanked them off script. He'd expected her to send him packing, so he'd prepared to beg. To his surprise, she seemed as eager to see him as he was her. And it appeared she also had something to say.

"I don't want one of us to lose in this, Rodrigo." She sounded conflicted but determined, and that only increased his hopes that things could work out. He was convinced that what he had in mind was the answer. And if she agreed with him, they could walk into the boardroom as a united front.

"Me, either." He ached to touch her, had to put his hands in his trouser pockets to keep from doing it. "We deserve this chance, both of us do, and I think I have a way to make it work, but first I need to say something." His voice almost gave out with those last words.

"You don't have to, Rodrigo, I—"

"Please, Joya. Let me say this to you," he pleaded. This felt like the most important moment of his life, the weight on his chest cementing that this conversation was the one that he *must* get right. He'd lost too much time by keeping what he felt locked inside. He'd let this woman who meant everything to him think he didn't care for her out of misguided loyalty. At the time he hadn't had many choices, but he had them now. He needed to make sure Esmeralda understood she'd never been anything less than essential. That he'd felt her absence in his life every single day of the past ten years.

"There is something I should've said about what happened at that meeting with Global Networks.

What I did, I didn't do that for me, for Sambrano or even just for you. I did it for us. Mi amor."

Those two words, *my love*. They fell from his lips so naturally, as if they had been on the tip of his tongue for years and were now rushing to be spoken. To her.

"In these past few years I lost my passion for the work. I have doggedly stayed on at Sambrano because I couldn't think of what else to do. But in the few days you've been here…" he said, taking her hands in his. Unable to hold back, he clutched them to his chest. "You've reminded me of the reasons I fell in love with this business. Of how even during those times when I wondered if I could continue dealing with the intrigue and the scheming, I couldn't walk away. And now I know why."

"Why?" Esmeralda asked breathlessly, as she pressed herself to him. If she was seeking his closeness then things could not be too far gone. Maybe there really was a chance for them. For a future together.

"I needed a partner. I needed someone who shared my vision of where we can take your father's legacy. Someone who understands what this company can be. I was waiting for *you*." He saw her eyes fill with tears, but there was a smile on her lips and a small ember of hope lit up in his chest. "I think we should both get to run Sambrano Studios." He watched as his words registered, and her smile grew a little bit wider.

"Both of us? But the board said they would pick. That only one person could have the job. How?"

He nodded at her questions, and with every passing second he was further convinced this was the path forward. That this was the only way they could have it all. The only way to ensure that the company was run in a way that honored Patricio's vision while giving their relationship a fighting chance.

"We split the position."

"Split it?" she asked, leaning back but never letting go of his hands.

"Yes." He nodded, hoping she'd agree. "President and CEO could very well be done by two people. The CEO is the person who manages operations, who has a handle on the business. I can do that. I've *been* doing that. But the president is all about vision, about keeping us looking at the bigger picture. That's you, Esmeralda."

Her brows furrowed in concentration, head tilted to the side as she considered his proposal. He knew this would mean asking her to trust him, and he hoped he hadn't shattered that completely. She hummed, and he smiled knowing this was the sound she made when she was lost in thought. She let go of his hands, but her expression wasn't forbidding—she was analyzing.

He felt the urgency under his skin. That electric feeling he only got when he knew he had a winner in his hands. In television these days it seemed like everything had been done. So many networks focusing on reboots and revivals of past hits. But every once in a while, something came across his desk that he knew could change the game. He had that feeling now.

When she finally looked up at him, there was a glint in those beautiful whiskey-colored eyes he hadn't seen in what felt like an eternity. Today she'd forgone the suit for something that was more Esmeralda. A dark green knee-length dress that managed to look professional and also highlight every luscious curve of her body. Her honey curls cascaded over her shoulders and when he looked closely he smiled at the sight of her lucky hoops dangling from her ears.

She stepped up, her eyes boring into him. "Before I agree to anything there are a few things I need to be very clear on, Rodrigo Almanzar. One..." She held up a finger, her other hand on her hip. "I will not be a silent partner. I want us to both have the same authority."

"Of course, I expect you to run this place with me."

"Two. I will have opinions, and I will have plans. Some of those will be different from yours or push against what you're envisioning and we will have to find ways to compromise. To figure out what works best for the company."

"A partnership," he agreed, his heart beating in his chest and a smile already tugging at his lips. He was usually careful, never one to count his eggs before they hatched, but it was hard to hold back when he was so close to getting everything he'd ever wanted.

"I refuse to just be a convenient warm body with the last name Sambrano that you trot out for photo ops." She was trying very hard to sound mad, but her lips were fully pulled up in a hopeful smile he could almost bet was a mirror image of his own.

"I expect you to be at the office across from mine every day and to help me build a network that we can both be proud of," he told her, and he tugged on her hand, bringing her a little closer.

"Are you really willing to take a pay cut?" she probed, this time her expression much more serious. He was. He'd thought about it and the reality was that going from making fifty million to twenty-five was almost an absurd thing to be upset about. And he barely spent on anything. Because he had no life. He'd paid cash for his house and the other properties were investments that essentially paid for themselves. It was a good thing, too, since most of the wealth he'd accumulated had gone into a stake in Sambrano. It had been worth every penny.

"Getting half of what I get now isn't exactly a hardship, mi vida." He was running fast and loose with the endearments, but he couldn't seem to stop himself. She was all that: his love, his life, his jewel. And it was about time he started saying it.

He brought her into his arms and she pressed into him like he was her harbor, her body relaxing against him. Soft and warm…and perfect. He would spend the rest of his life earning the right to be the shoulder she always leaned on. "Can we really do this? What if the board doesn't go for it?"

He pressed kisses into her hair, just because he needed to be as close as possible. "This board is interested in preserving the core values of this company, and once they see your presentation and hear *our* plan they won't be able to deny that this is the most logical path forward."

"But what about Carmelina?" He could not help the growl that rose from his throat at the mention of the woman.

"She's lost her power. Now she needs us to dictate what happens with Sambrano. The two of us together have more power than she does."

Esme looked up at him, her eyes bright with something that looked very much like his future and pushed up until their lips were pressed together. "I want this to work," she confessed against his lips.

"*We* will make it work. Because the most important part of this plan is you and me, and we already have that." They pressed their foreheads together as their mouths met again. Soon he was holding her tight. Deepening the kiss. Every cell in his body attuned to the woman in his arms. The only person on earth who could bring him back to himself. Who was able to remind him who he'd always wanted to be. The woman who brought into perfect clarity for him that success wasn't just about power—it was about turning that power into purpose.

Someone knocked on the glass door to his office, and when Esme went to step away from him he pressed her closer. He would die before hiding what this woman meant to him ever again.

"Sir, the board is ready for you," his assistant informed him and discreetly slipped out again.

"Are you ready for this?" Esmeralda asked as she gripped his hand and headed to the door. He looked down at her, overwhelmed by the rightness of the moment. The certainty in what they were about to do. "It feels like we've been waiting half our lives for this," she said, almost dreamily.

"Our future's waiting, mi amor. Let's go claim it," he said, as he walked out of his office with the love of his life by his side.

Epilogue

One Year Later

"Mmm… I love starting a workweek like this." Esmeralda gasped as Rodrigo trailed kisses down her body, his lips parting so he could lap at her heated skin.

"Technically we're off today, amor. Travel day," he reminded her before sucking one of her hard nipples into his mouth.

"Right," she responded, voice reedy with need. They were supposed to fly to Las Vegas in a few hours. They had a big week ahead of them, which had Esme a bit jittery, but Rodrigo's hands and mouth on her always had the power to make everything else feel inconsequential. Especially when his lips hovered right at her heat. She pulsed with need, desire coiling up inside her tighter and tighter until she was trembling from it.

"Mmm, here it is," he whispered as his fingers explored her. His tongue flicked her clitoris, making her cry out. "I love it when you scream for me, mi vida," he told her, voice low and dirty as he sucked and licked Esmeralda into a frenzy.

"I need you," she pleaded, widening her legs to make room for him, and soon he was sliding up her body, cock in his hand and about to enter her.

"Is this what you want?" he growled against her ear as he pressed the tip into her.

She gasped as pleasure threatened to obliterate her. "All of you, baby, please."

"I love you," he groaned as he pushed in slowly. He was a big man and even when she was burning for him she needed time to accommodate all of him. Sometimes she wanted slow, sweet lovemaking, and Rodrigo would do that. He'd keep her on the brink, pleasuring her again and again for hours, but this morning, she wanted it fast and hard. And he seemed to always know exactly what she wanted. In a couple of thrusts he sheathed himself in her. Filling her to the brim.

"You're perfect," he whispered against her mouth as he started to move. His hips circling in that way that made every nerve inside her spark. The heat of him always managed to melt her.

"We're perfect together." She gasped as she moved to meet him thrust for thrust. They'd come together a year ago and started building the life she'd always wanted and thought she would never be able to have. They were true and equal partners in everything. Even their home. As he moved in her, she pressed kisses to his skin, grateful for this man and this life she now had.

"Where did you go, baby? Am I not keeping your attention?" he teased and a pool of heat spread at her center as he brought his thumb to her mouth. "Get it wet for me, sweetheart." She shuddered out a shaky breath then sucked on it as he asked. Once he was satisfied he brought the pad of his finger down to her engorged clit and circled it exactly how he know she liked. Within seconds a frantic, electric wave of pleasure was crashing into her. He doubled his efforts, pistoning into her ruthlessly, and soon he was stiffening over her in a silent cry as his own climax took him.

He gathered her into his arms, as if she was something precious. As she burrowed into Rodrigo, Esme once again marveled at how different her life was now than it had been a year ago when she'd crashed into the Sambrano boardroom to claim her inheritance. After they'd walked into that meeting together and presented their plan to the board everything had fallen into place, almost as if fate had been waiting for the two of them to finally figure it out.

The board had not only approved splitting the

president and CEO position, they thought it was the ideal solution. And once that had been sorted out, Rodrigo and Esme began working on their relationship. And that had been a wonderful adventure, too. Last month they'd moved into their new home—a renovated brownstone in the Upper West Side that they'd bought together. And now she was lying in their master bedroom, which had a gorgeous view of the Hudson. She had everything she'd ever dreamed of. Including the man who had stolen her heart at twenty-one.

A kiss on her temple brought her out of her thoughts and Rodrigo's raspy morning voice in her ear made a shiver run through her. "What are you thinking?"

"That I'm happy, and nervous as hell for this week."

That earned her another kiss, this one deeper and hotter, the kind that made her toes curl and her heart flutter. "We got this, baby," Rodrigo whispered in her ear, as he shifted them so she was lying on top of him.

In her heart she knew they would be fine, but she was still nervous. Today they were headed to the International Broadcasters Trade Show, where Sambrano Studios would be unveiling their newest product: a streaming service package with four new networks solely producing Latinx content. Food and travel, history, music, and film and documentary channels celebrating every Latinx culture from

Mexico all the way to Argentina. Rodrigo and the board had let her run with her vision this past year, and now they were ready to make it public. The response from the beta trials had been wildly successful, but now her baby would be out there in the world.

"I hope people like it."

"It's brilliant," he said as he put a hand behind her head and brought her down for a kiss. His handsome, beloved face was open and bright as he smiled up at her—Rodrigo smiled so often now. "*You're* brilliant, and this is going to put the Sambrano brand on another level. You were what we needed. You were what *I* needed. The future is bright, mi cielo. And I can't wait to spend it with you."

"Te amo," Esmeralda said, her eyes filling with happy tears as she let the man she loved wrap her in his arms.

* * * * *

COMING NEXT MONTH FROM

DESIRE

#2815 TRAPPED WITH THE TEXAN

Texas Cattleman's Club: Heir Apparent • by Joanne Rock

To start her own horse rescue, Valencia Donovan needs the help of wealthy rancher Lorenzo Cortez-Williams. It's all business between them despite how handsome he is. But when they're forced to take shelter together during a tornado, there's no escaping the heat between them...

#2816 GOOD TWIN GONE COUNTRY

Dynasties: Beaumont Bay • by Jessica Lemmon

Straitlaced Hallie Banks is nothing like her superstar twin sister, Hannah. But she wants to break out of her shell. Country bad boy Gavin Sutherland is the one who can teach her how. But will one hot night turn into more than fun and games?

#2817 HOMECOMING HEARTBREAKER

Moonlight Ridge • by Joss Wood

Mack Holloway hasn't been home in years. Now he's back at his family's luxury resort to help out—and face the woman he left behind. Molly Haskell hasn't forgiven him, but they'll soon discover the line between hate and passion is very thin...

#2818 WHO'S THE BOSS NOW?

Titans of Tech • by Susannah Erwin

When tech tycoon Evan Fletcher finds Marguerite Delacroix breaking into his newly purchased winery, he doesn't turn her in—he offers her a job. As hard as they try to keep things professional, their chemistry is undeniable...until secrets about the winery change everything!

#2819 ONE MORE SECOND CHANCE

Blackwells of New York • by Nicki Night

A tropical destination wedding finds exes Carter Blackwell and maid of honor Phoenix Jones paired during the festivities. The charged tension between them soon turns romantic, but will the problems of their past get in the way of a second chance at forever?

#2820 PROMISES FROM A PLAYBOY

Switched! • by Andrea Laurence

After a plane crash on a secluded island leaves Finn Steele with amnesia, local resident Willow Bates gives him shelter. Sparks fly as they're secluded together, but will their connection be enough to weather the revelations of his wealthy playboy past?

YOU CAN FIND MORE INFORMATION ON UPCOMING HARLEQUIN TITLES, FREE EXCERPTS AND MORE AT HARLEQUIN.COM.

HDCNM0721

SPECIAL EXCERPT FROM

DESIRE

A tropical-destination wedding finds exes Carter Blackwell and maid of honor Phoenix Jones paired during the festivities. The charged tension between them soon turns romantic, but will the problems of their past get in the way of a second chance at forever?

Read on for a sneak peek at
One More Second Chance *by Nicki Night.*

"Listen." Carter broke the silence when they reached her door. "I didn't mean to upset you."

Phoenix cut him off. "Don't worry about it."

"I thought the timing was right. We were getting along and..."

"It's evident you still have an issue with timing," Phoenix snapped.

Her comment stung. Carter took a deep breath and exhaled slowly. He tried not to lose his patience with her.

"I'm sorry. I shouldn't have said that." Phoenix carefully stepped over the threshold and turned back toward Carter.

"I'm sorry, too. Hopefully we can move on. It was nice being friendly. Maybe one day we could go back to that."

Phoenix looked away. When she looked back at Carter, there was something unreadable in her eyes. Had she been more affected by his news than he realized? Their eyes locked. Carter felt himself moving closer to her.

"We just need to get through the wedding tomorrow and the next few days, and we can go back to living our normal lives.

You won't have to see me and I won't have to see you."

Phoenix's words struck something in him. He didn't like the idea of never seeing her again. The past few days had awakened something in him. Even the tense moments reminded him of what he once loved about her. He remembered his own words… *The way I love you.*

Carter kept his eyes on hers. She held his gaze. Old feelings returned, stirring his emotions. Perhaps those feelings had never left and remained dormant in his soul. His heart quickened. Desire flooded him and he wondered what Phoenix would do if he kissed her. She still hadn't looked away. Was she waiting for him to leave? Did she want to kiss him as much as he wanted to kiss her? Maybe she was having some of the same wild thoughts. Maybe old feelings were coming to the surface for her, too.

Carter stepped closer to Phoenix. She didn't move. Carter noticed the rise and fall of her chest become more intense. He stepped closer. She stayed put. He watched her throat shift as she swallowed. He smelled the sweet scent of perfume. He wondered if he could taste the salt on her skin.

Carter wasn't sure if it was love, but he felt something. It was more than lust. He missed Phoenix. The thought of her absence burned in him. In this moment he realized every woman since her had been an attempted replacement. That's why none of those relationships worked. But Phoenix would never have him. Would she?

HDEXP0721